EVERYONE
WAS THERE

D1263905

EVERYONE WAS THERE

———————————— *stories* ————————————

Anthony Varallo

www.elixirpress.com

Book design by Steven Seighman

Library of Congress Cataloging-in-Publication Data
Names: Varallo, Anthony, 1970-, author.
Title: Everyone was there : stories / Anthony Varallo.
Description: Denver, Colorado : Elixir Press, [2017]
Identifiers: LCCN 2017000609 | ISBN 9781932418637 (alk. paper)
Classification: LCC PS3622.A725 A6 2017 | DDC 813/.6--dc23
LC record available at https://lccn.loc.gov/2017000609

10 9 8 7 6 5 4 3 2 1

To Malinda, Gus and Ruby

ACKNOWLEDGMENTS

The author would like to thank the editors of the magazines where these stories first appeared:

AGNI: "Theft" and "Our First Couple"
AGNI Online: "The Boy," "The First Days," and "Sometimes She Wondered What Would Happen"
The Chattahoochee Review: "He Didn't Want to Talk About It" and "Falling Outs"
Cimarron Review: "Once You Learn, You Never Forget"
Denver Quarterly: "What a Night Sky"
Elsewhere: "When I Heard About the Trombone"
Epoch: "Question Man"
Fiction Southeast: "Monkeyshines"
Green Mountains Review: "We Knew the Children Had Arrived"
Gulf Coast: "Sleep"
Harvard Review: "Yearbook"
Harvard Review Online: "My Family Recalls a Cookout, Circa 1989"
Hobart: "7-Eleven" and "Wash Theory"
Hotel Amerika: "What I Would Tell the Squirrels"
Indiana Review: "My Enemy"
Juked: "The Bottom of This"
JuxtaProse: "Dispatches From a Housesitter"

Matchbook: "John Updike" and "Good Day"
Mid-American Review: "The Pinball Speaks"
NANO Fiction: "Yard Work" and "The Good Phone"
Newfound Journal: "Room History"
New World Writing: "The Fan"
Parcel: "Chutes and Ladders"
Passages North: "Was That The Time We Walked Through a Field or…?"
Pithead Chapel: "And Plus"
Puerto del Sol: "Horn Lessons, 1980"
Quarter After Eight: "What Did We Do To the Hardings?"
Quarterly West: "Can Opener vs. Mahler's Fifth"
Quick Fiction: "Hunger" and "Collecting"
The Southeast Review: "At Ease"
The Superstition Review: "Everyone Was There"
Southern Humanities Review: "A Glass of Coke"
StoryQuarterly: "Dummy"
Talking River: "A Possible Thing"
Twelve Stories: "Welding"
Vestal Review: "My Father Conducts Mahler's Ninth" and "The Inter-
section"
Weave: "All Very Surprising"
Western Humanities Review: "Not Stuart"
Word Riot: "He Could Play the Clarinet"
Wigleaf: "Unfriend" and "Bad Car"

CONTENTS

7-ELEVEN

When I was fourteen my mother moved into an apartment across town with my principal, Mr. Lorenzo, who was rumored to keep a pistol strapped beneath his dress slacks. My younger sister, Caroline, locked herself inside her bedroom. My older brother, Randy, joined a wannabe gang. My father took to staying up into the wee hours listening to big band records, a new and surprising habit that complicated my efforts to wish him goodnight, and convinced me never to mention that I had started seeing my mother and Mr. Lorenzo at the 7-Eleven near my school.

I saw them often. The first time, they were shoplifting ice cream novelties. Mr. Lorenzo held open one of the freezer doors while my mother filled her purse with Fudgsicles and Drumsticks. The second time, my mother played a video game as Mr. Lorenzo filled out a job application. The third time—but I ran away before they saw me spying from behind the hot dog carousel. I ran outside, where my brother's gang was trying, unsuccessfully, to break a bottle against the wall.

"Ragamuffin!" my brother shouted.

"We alarm you!" another gang member cried. He waved a knife he'd fashioned out of aluminum foil.

My father drank bourbon on those nights he listened to big band records. I got to know some of the numbers pretty good, well enough to say, "Which Dorsey is this?" something I'd rather say than, "I saw Mr.

Lorenzo and Mom making out in the 7-Eleven parking lot this morning." But my father didn't answer; he just sipped his bourbon and conducted the air with his fingers the way he sometimes did.

I realized this was a low time for our family.

And then Caroline turned into a bird. I heard her thrashing against her bedroom window, so I opened it and watched her fly off to wherever she flew off to. "Poor Caroline," I whispered, but really I was kind of jealous.

A few days later Mr. Lorenzo and my mother started working nights at the 7-Eleven. My mom wore a nametag that said, *Ask Me About Lotto Pick-Six!* Mr. Lorenzo manned the Slurpee machine. It got dark out, but my father never asked me where I was going or what I was up to, even when I replaced all his Benny Goodman records with sand.

And maybe I should have seen it coming, but I didn't.

One night my brother's gang tried to rob the 7-Eleven with swords they'd made from paper towel tubes, and Mr. Lorenzo shot Randy with his pistol. My mother screamed loud enough to wake Caroline, who'd made a little nest inside the 7 of the 7-Eleven sign. Caroline flew to our house and beat her wings against the window. She could see our father inside, listening to music, but all he heard was sand.

THE BOY

The boy's parents often told him that if he didn't stop misbehaving they'd leave the house without him. And one day, they did. "We tried to tell you," they said. They closed the front door and pulled out of the driveway. They neglected to wave goodbye. The boy watched them out the window. He'd never realized how funny his parents looked in their car before. Like little dolls. Or pets.

Years passed.

The boy grew. He trimmed the grass around the front walkway with the mower his father had left behind and mended clothes with his mother's sewing machine. Around the holidays he invited the neighbors over for hot cider and macaroons. "What happened to your parents?" the neighbors always meant to say, but never got around to somehow. They asked the boy for his macaroon recipe.

"It's from a mix," he admitted.

In high school the boy played varsity baseball and starred in the senior play. He met a girl who wore a ribbon in her hair and sometimes invited her back to his home, where he told her about his parents. The girl cried and kissed him and let the ribbon out of her hair. At night the boy played billiards at his father's pool table, the one the boy used to hide under when he was misbehaving. Or maybe the boy only imagined that. The thing was, he couldn't even remember what he'd done to drive his parents away. Something, he thought. He'd done something.

One day the boy was sitting in the recliner he'd recently recovered when his parents appeared in the doorway. There his father was; and there his mother was, too.

"What did you do to the recliner?" his father said.

The boy took their coats, which were wet with rain. "Would you two like something to drink?" the boy asked.

"We're not *guests*," his father said. He'd grown old; his voice shook. The boy got them some tea.

The three of them sat in the living room and drank tea. Light slanted in from the front windows, making long stripes across the room. The boy studied his parents. His mother was still pretty in her way, but older, heavier, her eyes refusing to meet his. His father wrung his hat in his hands—that same hat!—and regarded the room with clear disappointment. Clocks ticked. Occasionally cars passed outside, renewing the degree of silence between the three of them.

Finally the boy's father said, "We only wanted to teach you a lesson. You know? So you'd learn."

The boy's mother began to cry. "That's all we ever really wanted," she said. "Say you understand."

MY ENEMY

I saw my enemy today. He was in the car ahead of me, talking on his cell phone. He had his visor down and seemed to be observing himself within its square mirror. When he stopped at a red light, I could see my enemy's lips. They were small and thin, yet full of malice. The light changed; I honked my horn. "Let's go," I said. My enemy gave me a look, then pulled away. "Finally," I said. I was late for a dental appointment.

The appointment went well until my dentist introduced his new assistant, and I saw my enemy extend his sinister hand. "Hello," I said.

"Hello," my enemy said.

He went to work. "Let me know if you feel any sensitivity," my enemy said, and shoved a small harpoon into my gums. I could see my enemy's eyes, creepily glassed behind a safety mask. He scraped between molars and incisors. I felt pain shoot through my jaw, but didn't say anything. I tasted blood. My enemy smiled.

I spent the rest of the morning at work, responding to emails. An entire page of email carried the same subject line: "BUSINESS PROPOSAL." I opened one and read my enemy's propaganda. *Dear Who It May Concern,* the message began, *a fortune of high importance awaits you as the benefactor of the heir of the Schulyerhazy dynasty,* etc, etc. *Dear Prince Schulyerhazy,* I wrote, *what would you know about sensitivity?* I clicked "send" and left work early.

On the way home I stopped by the supermarket. I wanted those little pretzels shaped like wagon wheels, but I couldn't find them. An employee was shelving potato chips, and it wasn't until he'd turned to answer my question that I realized my enemy was moonlighting as a grocery clerk. "They don't make those anymore," he lied. His acne was hideous. When I left the aisle, I glimpsed my enemy shelving the pretzels where I'd already looked.

When I arrived home, my trash cans were scattered across the driveway; my enemy had stolen the lids. He'd craftily placed them on top of his trash cans as if I wouldn't notice. "Oh, I noticed," I said, as I returned them to their rightful places. "I noticed all right."

That night the phone rang in the middle of my favorite television show. "Hello," my enemy's voice said. "I hope I'm not calling at a bad time, sir, but I wanted to inform you about a special low-interest credit—"

"Listen," I interrupted. "If you touch my trash cans again I'll break your neck."

"Sir?"

"And I found the pretzels," I said.

My enemy paused, then whispered, "Where?"

"Behind the Doritos."

"Next time I'll hide them better," my enemy said.

"You're a lousy dental assistant," I said.

"I'll steal your teeth!" my enemy hissed, but I'd already hung up.

WE KNEW THE CHILDREN
HAD ARRIVED

When the first buses pulled into the neighborhood, we knew the children had arrived. We saw the buses through half-open windows where we sat with our husbands and wives, aunts and uncles, pets, newspapers and radios. We stood from kitchen tables, pointed outside. We felt our hearts beating in our ears. We made hasty plans. Lock the doors, we said. Call the police.

But no one did anything. We watched the buses slow to the curb, where they idled for a few moments before the front doors swung open and the children began to descend. Their sneakers made tiny sucking sounds upon the sidewalk.

We huddled together, held hands. Don't move, we whispered. Maybe they won't—

But they did. The children knocked. We heard them laughing their childish laughter. We heard them smacking gum.

"Don't make us huff and puff," they said.

When we heard windows breaking and garage doors rolling up, one after another, like a sudden thunderstorm, we knew the children had arrived.

"You knew this day was coming," they said. They wore baggy shorts and oversized T-shirts. Occasionally they took breaks from beating us with loose boards to send text messages. Their fingers worked furiously across their iPhones and BlackBerrys, and then they put their iPhones and

BlackBerrys away and hauled us into our front yards where, already, piles of our most cherished possessions lay burning in tall heaps.

"This can't be a surprise," the children said. They ordered us into files, from weakest to strongest. They ordered us to undress, tossing our sweaty clothes onto the burning fires, which sent a thick smoke into the sky. They ridiculed our footwear. We shivered and wept.

"We always said we'd be back," they said.

When the bus doors opened and we felt ourselves being pushed inside, fifty to a bus, seventy-five, one hundred, and could no longer distinguish our tears from our neighbors' tears, our screams from our neighbors' screams, we knew the children had arrived. And, when the buses pulled onto the highway, where they were joined by a thousand other buses, all heading from neighborhoods burning against the evening sky, we not only knew the children had arrived; we understood.

AT EASE

My senior year of high school I went to the prom with a girl whose boyfriend had been killed in Iraq. Donald, the boyfriend's name was. I'd met him a few times before he was shipped out. He'd come to school with Vicki (that's the girl I went to the prom with, Vicki) back when we were juniors and he was away in training. Donald had worn his full regalia: razor-pleated pants, a stiff white shirt, shoes polished so thoroughly they looked like black glass. He stood in lunch line with us and let the cafeteria workers pile his tray high with mound after mound of terrible food. "Much appreciated, ma'am," he said. Or, "Now *that's* what I call cookin.'" You could see how much the workers loved him. I know; I was standing right behind him. Under the heat lamps, Donald's skin exuded the smell of halved limes.

The night of the prom I drove to Vicki's house. Her parents took pictures of us standing in front of the fireplace. A little white dog breathed hot air on my socks until Vicki's mother scooped him up and deposited him outside. Vicki's little brother, Raymond Jr., pointed at me like I was an intruder. "Donald!" he said, a second before Vicki's father dragged him into the kitchen. "We're sorry," Vicki's mother said. But she had already started to cry. Vicki looked away. I felt my face grow hot.

The prom theme was "New York, New York." They'd decorated the gymnasium to look like the city skyline, including the World Trade Center. There'd been a debate about whether to include the World

Trade Center or not; the school paper ran a million editorials. They'd strung the towers with lights shaped like crosses.

"Jesus," Vicki sighed.

"Yeah," I said. "Jesus."

During slow dances I held Vicki away; she didn't seem to mind. We sat out the fast songs, hanging out at a table with a group of friends. Someone passed around a bottle of Jim Beam. Vicki took large swallows like they were nothing at all. People gave me looks, but I wasn't sure what the looks meant. Later, we danced another slow song, but this time Vicki pulled me closer. I could feel her breasts against my chest. I must have acted nervous because I thought I heard Vicki say something, but when I looked at her she had her eyes closed. *At ease*, she'd said.

That night I drove Vicki home. We sat in her driveway, not saying anything. All the houselights were off, the night starry. I put my hand to Vicki's knee, her thigh. I'd never done anything like that before. I heard Vicki breathe. I permitted my hand to ascend. I'd never done that before, either. And it was like it all started when Vicki said those words to me.

ALL VERY SURPRISING

What were the chances her baby would be born talking?

"Slim," the baby said. He had just unburdened himself of his hospital blanket, which fell from his pink shoulders and exposed the umbilical stump still clinging to his belly button. "They don't give you a big enough blanket, do they?" he said. He offered her a toothless smile. "Oh, already I seem to feel the chill of death!" he intoned.

His mother began to cry. They'd been home from the hospital one week, and already she'd given up trying to understand.

"Please don't cry, mother dear," the baby said. "For I am prone to melodrama."

The mother lived alone, her husband gone, her house fitted out with the rocking chair, bassinet, crib, changing table, Pack 'n Play, and books and toys her mother had purchased secondhand for her. "Don't show up at my doorstep one day," her mother warned. "Understand? I've given you what you needed and I'll continue to give you what you need, but don't show up at my doorstep one day."

"I won't show up at your doorstep one day," she said, but her mother only laughed.

"Always the last to know," she said.

At night the mother bathed the baby in the plastic bathtub she was able to fit inside the kitchen sink. She rinsed the baby with the detachable sink nozzle, the baby neglecting to close his eyes as she maneuvered the spray above his head. In the bathwater, the baby looked suddenly tender and helpless, and the mother found herself whispering, "I love you," as she shielded his eyes from lather. The baby gave her a curious look and said, "What is your definition of love, mother dear?"

The mother stopped rinsing him and cleared her throat. "Well," she said, and then offered several explanations cribbed from popular songs and movies and the few Bible verses she could vaguely recall from her childhood. The baby nodded without comment. But later, when she was slipping him into his onesie, the baby said, "You know, I wasn't very impressed with your definition." The mother rocked him in the rocking chair and read him the books her mother had chosen: *Goodnight, Moon; If You Give a Mouse a Cookie; Guess How Much I Love You; Go Dog, Go.* She thought the baby might be nodding off, but he only shook his baby head and said, "These books are full of lies, aren't they?" He gave her a look. "And me so wee and glee."

Mornings, the mother took her baby to Starbucks, where people gave her looks for placing a sippy cup of iced macchiato in the stroller's beverage holder. She sped the stroller through the door. "If there's one thing I simply cannot abide in a barista," the baby said, sucking noisily on the macchiato, "it's chuffiness."

Afternoons, they went to Target, where the mother picked up some diapers and wipes, and checked items in the clearance aisle. "Savings," the baby said, inspecting the garden tools at stroller height. "More like the *idea* of savings, right-o, mother dear?" A woman approached them and knelt down to see the baby. "Ooh, what a cutie patootie we have here!" she said. "With a wittle face that's so squeezy-weezy! Ooh, yes it is, yes it is!" She held his face as if it were a rare and delicate fruit. When she was out of earshot, the baby said, "What is the sorrow that drives her?"

One evening the mother put the baby in his car seat and carried him to the car, which had already been packed with boxes of baby clothes, toys, the plastic bathtub, the stroller, and the Pack 'n Play hastily folded into its carrying sack. "Oh, but I am an unwanted puppy en route to a strange farm!" the baby said. The mother began to cry. "I'm sorry," she said, "it's just that this is all—" and she gave way to sobbing.

"It's just that this is all very surprising," the baby offered.

The mother nodded, and began to wail.

"Don't cry, mumsy," the baby said, "for there is no end to all the very surprising things, is there?"

The mother was about to answer when the sky opened up and rain began to fall.

"Ah, who knows the caprices of the weather?" the baby said.

When the mother arrived at her mother's house, she placed the baby in the stroller and pushed him to the doorstep, where she would leave him with the boxes, bathtub, Pack 'n Play, the crib, and all the other items her mother had purchased for her. The rain had picked up; the mother fastened a canopy over the stroller and pulled it low. "How the winds do blow, mommy-o!" the baby said. "So suiting our current mood!" The mother leaned beneath the canopy and kissed the baby on his head. His skin tasted faintly of old milk. The baby's eyes met hers. "Believe you can do it, me mutter; believe it as best you can."

And she'd nearly made it out of the neighborhood when the storm worsened; rain slapped her windshield like a rebuke. Would the canopy hold? She circled back to her mother's house, saw the stroller on the doorstep with its canopy bucking in the wind, and saw, as clearly as she saw the years lengthening before her, where she would raise this baby into childhood, adolescence, and adulthood, that, as much as she'd like to imagine she could deposit her baby into her mother's care, she could never really leave such matters to chance.

HUNGER

At night I like to eat pretzels out of a little green bowl. I keep the bowl in a cabinet above the stove along with other bowls, plates, and coffee mugs. The bowl has a small chip on the bottom. I don't really notice the chip anymore, except for when I'm taking the bowl out of the dishwasher, where the bowl rests upside down on the top rack. Then I remember it. I usually run the little green bowl through the dishwasher every other night or so. It depends. If I need the bowl and the dishwasher isn't full enough to run, I'll take the bowl out and wash it by hand. I make sure to wash it clean.

Once the bowl is ready I place it on the kitchen table and get the pretzels from the pantry. The pretzels are those mini-sized ones, small enough to put in your mouth all at once. I open the bag and scoop a handful of pretzels into the green bowl. I know I could just as easily tip the bag to the bowl and pour the pretzels in, but I don't like doing that. I like arranging them just a bit, so that I get as many pretzels as possible inside the bowl. It's amazing how many pretzels fit inside the little bowl. You wouldn't think that many would fit. But they do. I lift the bowl and take it into the living room. I turn the television on, settle onto the sofa, and place the little bowl of pretzels on the coffee table. That's my favorite part about eating pretzels from the little green bowl: placing the bowl on the coffee table as the television comes on.

My father, in the weeks before he died, spent nights watching television in his favorite chair, a brown corduroy recliner. Next to the chair he kept a large plastic jar of cashew nuts with a wide plastic top. The kind of jar you see at Costco or Sam's Club. Whenever I came to visit, which wasn't often and something I'd later regret, he'd offer me cashews from the plastic jar. I always said no. I don't know why, really. The truth was, I really wanted some. But I never accepted. Instead, we'd watch television together until it grew dark outside, my father reaching into the jar every now and then for another cashew. He had this way of eating them where he'd bite the cashew in half while holding the other half with his fingers, sniffing it, just for a second, on the sly. Then he'd eat the other half and repeat the whole thing again. We watched ballgames, sitcoms, evening news. But all I was thinking about were the cashews. Why had I turned them down? I wanted them more than anything.

CHUTES AND LADDERS

In going up the ladders and down the chutes a child will learn by pictures the rewards of doing good deeds and the consequences of naughty ones.
—FROM THE *CHUTES AND LADDERS* GAME INSTRUCTIONS

CHUTE: Cookie jar, broken, teeters from a high countertop. Below: boy, standing on a three-legged footstool, reaches inside. Crumbs freckle the floor.

LADDER: Boy, wearing red baseball cap, helps elderly woman across busy intersection. Driver in nearest car offers friendly wave. Elderly woman waves back. Boy's face radiates a clear lack of embarrassment.

CHUTE: Girl, seated before mirror, applying eye shadow. Mother, watching from doorway, arms folded. Note girl's look of surprise.

LADDER: Girl, kneeling before bed, praying. Girl's hands are clasped in a reverent, but non-denominational way. Open window admits a heavenly moon.

CHUTE: Teen, wearing polo shirt and khaki pants, leans in to accept a cigarette from teen in jean jacket. Nearby teen crowd looks on, predominately jean jacket wearers, smokers. Three stand before the open hood of a Camaro, nodding. Camaro is custom-painted. Flames. Skulls.

LADDER: Teen, wearing reflective sash, tours parking lot with trash bag and trash picking device. Device is shaped like a harpoon. Two cigarette butts—one still unsafely smoldering—lie impaled upon its prong. Teen inspects these like rare worms. Frowns.

CHUTE: Teenage girl, lying on canopy bed, speaks enthusiastically into a rotary telephone, laughing. Across the bed, textbooks with important spines—ALGEBRA, HISTORY, SHAKESPEARE—wait unopened. Nearby clock indicates that it is nearly eight-thirty p.m.

LADDER: Teenage girl, seated before smiling nurse, receives a bandage across her arm. A plate of donuts rests beside the girl, above which a sign hangs: BLOOD DRIVE. Donuts appear unusually large. Powdered.

CHUTE: Two boys, each with fishing rods, crouch behind a large, leafy tree. Man, wearing overalls, stands with hands cupped to his mouth, from which jagged lines ascend. The boys restrain considerable laughter. A handwritten sign, nailed to the tree, turns loosely in the wind: POSTED: NO FISHING.

LADDER: Boy, standing by large trash barrel, smiles at other boy, whose arms clutch a remarkably large pile of autumn leaves. Pyramids of carefully raked leaves testify to boys' superior raking skills and commendable lack of horseplay. Old man, seated on porch, watches, visibly pleased. Weatherboard sign hanging from porch: NURSING HOME.

CHUTE: Ant, crawling across non-specific surface, slumps within narrow circle of intense light. Boy, crouched behind surface, holds skillet-sized magnifying glass. The sun, faceless, conveys disappointment nonetheless.

LADDER: Boy's face, framed by ant farm, swells with excitement as teacher urges tiny ant inside. Boy's head is haloed by a half-dozen other faces, dazzled, awed. Girl, sporting large bow, clasps hands to cheeks, possibly screaming. Tiny ant, upon closer inspection, wears tiny grin.

CHUTE: Boys, girls, and teens sit gloomily around large rectangular table, visibly bored.

LADDER: Boys, girls, and teens happily join hands around large rectangular table, upon which colorful board game rests, emitting blinding, preternatural light. Game box reveals name.

THE PINBALL SPEAKS

I want to start by saying thank you, first and foremost, for this opportunity to address you all this evening. Please know how much I enjoyed meeting with many of you this afternoon; our conversation accompanied me, quite happily, to the lovely restaurant we hastily fled a few moments ago, my good host checking his watch and reminding me, without the least trace of panic, that we were already running late. He is a kind man, as I'm sure you know, who will certainly be embarrassed to hear himself included in this address; I see him blushing now. Forgive me my tardiness, sir. It is a pinball's habit to linger.

Thankfully, I was able to review a few of the questions you've supplied, at my request. These questions will help guide my observations, whose first is that a pinball needs to be steered, whether by bumper, flipper, or punctual host, and rarely seeks to chart his or her own course. A quality that may explain, in part, pinball's loss of popularity in recent years, along with the computer chip. The few children who peer at me beside their parent's gleeful faces now wear expressions of sheer boredom and pity, something I'll never quite grow used to somehow. A pinball rolls on and on, but is slow to change.

But a gloomy present cannot eclipse a glorious past. And what a past it was! I can still remember the days of steady work, when no sooner had I dropped between the flippers than I was released again from the plunger— whoosh!—the glass sky above me freckled with cigarette ash and the foam of root beer floats. An old pinball remembers root beer, pocket combs, and the crinkle of leather jackets.

But—onward. You've asked me how I feel about being a pinball, an odd question, sort of like asking how you feel about being, say, a mammal. The truth is I do not really know how I feel about being a pinball, and feel myself to be somewhat of a mystery to myself, if that's not too ridiculous to say. I am a composite of contradictions, to be sure: slow but fast, brave but fearful, a doer who is done unto, my front my back and my back my front. But these warring essences lend little complexity to my sense of self: I am a pinball. Guide me well. Never let me drop.

You've asked how I got my start, and must forgive me when I say I have no idea, really, my earliest recollection the same as last evening's: I was in darkness, then sped toward the light. I careened, I caromed; I dropped into darkness again. A pinball sees the religious in everything.

But I will tell you a secret, since tonight seems the occasion for secrets. When a pinball is in darkness, and the light seems far away, a pinball sometimes weeps and weeps. Listen closely, and you'll hear.

UNFRIEND

This morning my high school football coach follows me to work, where he paces in front of my desk while I'm on a conference call. He's grown older and heavier, but still has the habit of twisting his visor in his hands, as he did whenever we trailed at halftime. "You mind telling me one thing," he says, at the exact moment I'm the closest I've been to making this deal. I raise a finger, as if to say, *One moment*, but my coach ignores me. "Just tell me what gives you the right. That's all. What gives you the goddamned *right?*"

I'm about to answer, when my ex-wife's maid of honor joins the conference call. "You son of a bitch," she says. "After I sent you all those pictures of my kids' Christmas pageant." I'm about to tell her it didn't have anything to do with the pictures, but she cuts me off and says, "Save it. Okay? Just save it." I can hear her beginning to cry. "And here I was thinking I was being nice, what with everything that happened after you and Amelia split." I haven't heard her cry since the one time she called me after the divorce and told me she'd had a falling out with Amelia and I told her I would see what I could do, but ended up not mentioning it to Amelia, since my chief means of corresponding with Amelia had devolved into sending one another photos of salads we'd just made.

"I didn't mean to—" I say, but before I can finish, my office door swings open and my college roommate's lab partner bursts in and throws a Ralph Nader baseball cap at me, one that matches the T-shirt he's wearing and, I notice as he approaches my desk with an angry stride, a constellation of buttons and pins dotting his messenger bag. "Poser!" he shouts, and I can see the space between his front teeth that often imprisoned sunflower seeds. He clutches the edge of my desk, where the Nader cap has landed atop my iPod dock. "But this is what I'd expect from someone who voted Kerry!" he hisses. His breath is redolent of tapenade.

I escape to the men's room, but my neighbor's brother—the one who keeps sending me links to est conferences—is just finishing up at a urinal, while my father's Al-Anon's sponsor wrestles a paper towel from the wall dispenser, and says, "For your father's sake, I wish you'd reconsider." I head for the nearest stall, but my junior high yearbook editor is already inside, arms folded, staring me down with a clear look of contempt. "The sad part is," he says, in the slow, measured cadence he now uses in his audio posts, "I was always the one who defended you when everybody else said how shallow you were." The occupants of the other two stalls—my coworker's Wiccan sister and the Emo kid who bartends our company parties, respectively—punch and kick and call me names I'd hear if my driver's ed teacher wasn't yelling at me for not responding to his epic poem. "Sing, oh goddess," he cries, "of my murderous rage!"

I run to the lobby—my sixth grade pen pal pelting me with wadded airmail envelopes—and manage to reach the security desk before my sister's boyfriend grabs my sleeve and tells me I can just forget about checking out the Dave Matthews Band the next time they're in town. He's wearing the skinny jeans he and my sister posted photos of, and I would mention that I voted for the other, less-distressed pair, if the woman who always sends me links to her Etsy site didn't have me by the collar, her clunky and frightening and ill-wrought earrings juddering with unmistakable anger. "Don't think you'll be missed!" she says. "Because you won't."

Outside, it is raining, and I would take a cab to the subway if the cabs weren't driven by guys from my ex-wife's company softball team. So, I run to the subway, where half my senior class is pushing through the turnstiles, fists raised, and my mother's friend's son—the one whom my mother promised I'd give free drum lessons to—tries to take me out at the knees. I hurdle him, but cannot escape the crowd of poker buddies from my last job who gain on me as I reach the train, its interior crammed with my sister's graphic novel book club, my neighbor's best friend's adorable baby, that guy who always says hi to me at company barbecues, my land-lord's wife's physical therapist, and the members of the 1998 Greenfield High School Model UN Reunion Committee. They glare at me as I step onto the train. They hurl insults, damp umbrellas.

And I nearly make it to my seat, when someone pulls me by the hand. I turn to see my ninth grade girlfriend, privately the only person I believe I've ever loved, her pretty hair and face rain-soaked enough that I cannot tell whether she is crying or not when she asks me *why, when we said we'd stay good friends?*

SOMETIMES SHE WONDERED
WHAT WOULD HAPPEN

Sometimes she wondered what would happen if he found out. He would be angry, of course; there'd be no getting around that. He'd be furious. He'd say things he didn't really mean, the way he always did when they fought. He'd say he couldn't believe she could do this to him. How could she possibly do this to him? Why was she always doing things like this to him? Had she ever stopped to *think* about it? That's what he would want to know: had she ever really *just stopped* and *thought* about all the ways she'd failed him? He'd list several ways. He'd give examples. He was fond of giving examples, as in, "it's just like the time you wouldn't give that woman her Susan B. Anthony dollar back after you found it in the ashtray," or, "it's just like the time I asked you if you'd mailed the kitty food and you'd left it in Sarasota," or, "this is what I'd expect from someone who steals cable."

Then he'd sulk. God, how he would sulk if he found out! He'd grab his jacket and leave the house in a huff. He'd slam the door—whump!—and return an hour later, unable to think of anything to do that could match the degree of his anger. Later, he'd drink a few beers from the fridge, listen to music on headphones, making the angry face he always made when he drank beer and listened to music on headphones. He'd sleep on the sofa and leave the television on. When she said goodnight, he would pretend not to hear. He'd flip channels, watching all the shows she hated most. Shows she knew he didn't like either, like *CSI* or *The*

Girls Next Door. The next day he'd leave the house before her, hoping she'd worry.

But sometimes she didn't wonder what would happen if he found out, and then she'd feel okay. The two of them would go to a movie, or a bookstore, or the farmer's market, and she wouldn't think the least thing about what would happen if he found out. They would talk, make jokes, laugh. Days would pass. Weeks. They'd fall into the happy-ish routine they'd always known. They'd eat too many Indian buffets and visit his family in Arkansas. They'd make love. So much time would pass that she would wake up some mornings feeling cheery and hopeful, almost giddy, but then she would remember and the feeling would vanish and she'd wonder what would happen if he found out.

WELDING

When I was a kid, I missed a lot of school. Some days I just didn't feel like going. Other days I was sick. Colds. Stomachaches. I was always getting stomachaches. Or I hadn't done my homework. Fractions. Don't ask me about fractions. Some days I'd get dressed for school, tie my shoes, heave my book bag across my shoulder, but find myself unable to open the front door. I'd just stand there, ready to go, but not going. I could hear cars passing on the street outside.

On the days I stayed home I watched TV. There wasn't that much else to do. I'd fill a bowl of cereal and eat it while watching *The Price is Right* or the *Today Show*. The TV was one of those old console ones you now see in thrift stores; the kind where, just walking by, you can sense all the misery the TV was asked to witness, year after year, including, in my case, all those times I sat in front of ours with a bowl of Trix when I should have been at school mastering fractions. There was no remote, either; you had to commit to your choice, at least for a little while. Up close, the TV gave off a faint smell like burnt wax.

It was usually in the early afternoon, after I'd switched from VHF to UHF to avoid all the soap operas, that the welding commercial came on. *Do you have what it takes?* a voice would announce, as the commercial showed men and women putting on welding masks. *Get certified in less than six months!* the voice would say, and then the commercial focused on a solitary welder holding a bright torch to a shiny pipe. The welder wore dark coveralls and heavy work boots. Red sparks rained down upon his mask. When the camera drew close, the welder removed his mask and said, "Learn welding. It's a good job with good pay."

Whenever the welder said those lines, I always snapped the TV off. The afternoon sun suddenly made the room feel hot. No cars passed outside. I tried to do my homework, but it was no use. I couldn't concentrate on anything. I began to sweat. I kept hearing the welder say those lines. *Learn welding. It's a good job with good pay.* Like he was trying to tell me something.

Like there was something about me he knew.

GOOD DAY

I t had been a good day, they both agreed. Their sons had slept in, for once. For breakfast they had blueberry pancakes—they'd forgotten all about those blueberries—and their youngest son, Max, was finally able to drink from a glass without a straw. A fat cardinal materialized at the bird feeder outside the kitchen window, something that hadn't happened since forever.

"Look," their oldest son, Henry, said.

"Birdy bird," Max said.

They read the paper, which had arrived early today, and wasn't lawn-soaked, the way it usually was. Forecast: sunny. Dow: up. Coupons: abundant.

Such a good day, they went to the zoo. The zoo! They toured the reptile house and the monkey park. They saw the baby otters they'd seen on the news. "Remember? We saw them on the news," they said, and Max and Henry pressed their faces to the glass, as if peering into television itself.

"They're ugly," Henry said.

They'd stopped for lunch at Friendly's. They never stopped for lunch anymore. Their waitress seemed to know this, and brought Max and Henry crayons, coloring books, paper hats, and two chocolate milks before taking their order. Later, when they were finishing their fries, the waitress brought the children two butterscotch sundaes and handed them each a slender spoon. "Congratulations," she said. "You're sitting in the free sundae booth!"

In the afternoon, they watched *Cars* for the millionth time, although the jokes seemed suddenly new. Poor Lightning McQueen, never winning his Piston Cup! The mail arrived, a package from the boys' grandparents: two T-shirts and a rare Thomas train the boys' father hadn't been able to find anywhere. Max fell asleep on the family room sofa. Henry watched the bonus features. They were able to pick up all the towels from the bathroom floor.

After dinner they allowed the boys to play Wii, something they wouldn't normally have done, but this was a good day, after all—plus the boys kept begging. Max steered a skateboard across a collapsing bridge. Henry urged Mario through a volcano and discovered a hidden room. The room was filled with gold flowers, talking stars, and smiling mushrooms. Mario placed these in his pockets.

That night the boys brushed their teeth without instruction. Max mastered the idea of pajamas: you have to point your toes to get your feet through. Henry refused his Batman nightlight. They read the boys stories and said goodnight.

But, when the good day drew to a close, they found they could not sleep. Their bedroom felt too cold and too hot. They forgot to lock the basement door. Dogs barked. Max cried out. Henry followed. A thunderstorm arrived and crept into their dreams. They pulled the sheets to their chins, and felt the bad night descend.

EVERYONE WAS THERE

E veryone. Even the new barber, whose name no one could remember.
He drank three margaritas and praised Louise Fenton's lousy spinach
dip. The kid who rides his mini-bike on the sidewalk was there, too. He
played video games with the Hines' children and even let them try on
those fingerless gloves he's always wearing. No one said anything about
him riding on the sidewalk. It didn't seem right to say anything about
him riding on the sidewalk, especially with everyone being there, like Father Hearn and Mrs. Brofski and the Alexanders, including Rita, finally
back from Singapore and chatting happily with Julianna Meer, who was
also there and whom no one could recall acting so cheerful, especially
since the incident with Norman Brigantine, who was there, too, and who
seemed to be avoiding Julianna, departing a good hour before anyone else
and leaving his Philadelphia Eagles bottle opener on the credenza.

Gordon McLain pocketed the opener and later gave it to Mary Hedg-
es, who was also there, although not with Rick, but Peter Bennett, who
took the opener from Mary and was glad to assist Muriel Masters with a
tricky cider bottle when everyone was wondering what the woman who
never leaves the post office was doing there, clearly having left the post office and clearly having done something dramatic to her hair, which spilled
loosely from a white bow.

Several teenagers were there; too, the ones whom everyone suspected
of spray-painting BLOW ME! on the Hogarth's driveway (also there)

although they seemed polite enough, laughing at Colin Kiefer's off-color jokes and retrieving paper towels for the ghost of Billy Zimmer when he spilled Tanqueray on the sectional.

The girls-who-seem-to-be-in-Girl-Scouts-but-aren't-really were also there, huddled by the stairway, still wearing their phony sashes and stolen caps, making small talk with the UPS driver, Reggie, who was also there, along with Reggie's assistant, Jerome, who wore cracked Ray-Bans and never spoke a word. Chris Fitzsimmons was also there, as were Sheila Brown, Stephanie D'Amato, Greg Mackowski, and the girl who drives a golf cart around the cul-de-sac, Chloe. Around midnight an entire swim team showed up and joked noisily in the front foyer. Dr. Timins was also there. He drank nothing and eyed the swim team with clear disapproval. He didn't so much as nod to Colonel Wallace, who was also there, although without his parrot, Rutherford B. Hayes.

The event was so unprecedented, so spectacular, so full of fellowship, love, and community, that everyone went home feeling quite certain that, although they could not say what the occasion was, or who was hosting, or what street it was on, or whose home, or why any of them had gathered at all, everyone was there, everyone in the world.

THE FIRST DAYS

The first days the baby sleeps in a laundry basket.
"Isn't that kind of dangerous?" the father asks, but what does he know? This is his—their—first child. The father is nervous. The father has never been so nervous about anything. "It was in the book," the mother explains. But the baby won't fall asleep in the laundry basket.

The basket is cracked at one end, asked, too many times, to hold wet towels while the father rests the basket against his car, searching for keys. The mother and father have no washer and dryer and must drive to the Laundromat. The first days the father washes seventeen loads of wash.

At night, they take turns soothing the baby. This baby can cry. This baby arches his back and screams, red-faced, his baby fists clenched tight.

"What does the book say?" the father asks. But the mother is sleeping. The first days they sleep when they can. The first days the mother dreams of linen.

The father and the baby have a nighttime routine. The father holds the baby against his chest and bounces on the bed where the mother sleeps, all the while watching the lone tree limb visible through the bedroom window. The father likes this limb, and believes the baby does, too, for the baby has twice fallen asleep whenever the father narrowed his attention to the limb's branches, which catch the moonlight in pleasing ways. The baby's breath grows deeper, slower. The first days the mother wakes to find the father bouncing, eyes closed.

The first seventeen loads of laundry, the father checks inside the dryer to make sure he hasn't accidentally thrown the baby in, too. A preposterous fear, he knows, probably from a lack of sleep, but still. The first days the father watches *Oprah* on the Laundromat TV.

"Maybe we should call the doctor about his poop," the mother says, inspecting a diaper. The baby nurses at her chest. "It doesn't look like the poop in the book."

The father picks up the book, searches the index for *poop*. "What's it under?" he says. The first days the book rests atop the TV.

Sometimes the moonlight makes the tree branch look fantastically bright. How has the father never noticed how bright moonlight really is? The first days the father sees one owl and three bats outside the window.

One night the baby finally falls asleep in the basket.

"The book was right," the mother whispers.

"I've always liked that book," the father says.

On the eighteenth load of laundry, the father does not check inside the dryer. He removes the clothes and folds them into the basket. And it does not occur to him as he reaches the parking lot, where he must balance the basket against the car, that the first days are gone, and have become the next.

JOHN UPDIKE

John Updike didn't want to be a writer; he wanted to draw cartoons. When John Updike was twelve years old, he sent his first cartoon to *The New Yorker* (they rejected it). When he was twelve years old, a dogwood tree leaned against John Updike's home in Shillington, Pennsylvania. Shillington is a frequent setting for John Updike's short stories, sometimes renamed "Olinger." Olinger should be pronounced with a hard *g* sound, John Updike once explained. It is difficult to tell if John Updike's alter ego, Henry Bech, should be pronounced with a hard *c* sound, as in "peck," or a soft *c*, as in "bench." John Updike often slept in late, saying he preferred that "someone else start the world for him." When someone else read John Updike's work, they usually read *Rabbit, Run*; when John Updike read his own work, he usually read his poetry. Critics of John Updike often complained about his characterization of women and self-conscious prose. "John Updike has nothing to *say*," they said. The one time I met John Updike, he signed my book and said, "I hope you won't sell this on Ebay." John Updike is the only writer to have a short story reprinted in six consecutive decades of *The Best American Short Stories*. In one of my favorite John Updike stories—from the first John Updike collection I ever purchased—John Updike describes a snowy parking lot crisscrossed with tire tracks as "a blackboard in reverse." The John Updike Society recently purchased John Updike's childhood home for $180,000, with plans to turn it into a museum. In John Updike's short story, "Museums and Women," the narrator compares his first wife to a "room of porcelain vases: you enter and find your sense of yourself abruptly clarified by a cool, shapely expectancy in the air." David Foster Wallace said that John Updike wrote like *a penis with a thesaurus*. The time I met him, John Updike wore a red tie and a brown sportcoat. John Updike wrote his first novel, *The Poorhouse Fair*, in less than three months. *The Poorhouse Fair* is set in the town where John Updike grew up and will likely be mentioned during the museum tour of his childhood home. I did not tell John Updike how much I admired his writing; instead, I told him I liked a story of his in a recent *New Yorker*. "Oh, but that's a story I've written several times before, isn't it?" John Updike laughed. A tribute piece to John Updike is nothing new; Nicholson Baker wrote a memoir, *U and I*, about John Updike. (John Updike liked it.) John Updike did not learn to swim until he was in college. Usually I don't tell writer friends how much I like John Updike. John Updike had a slight stutter. John Updike won two National Book Awards and two Pulitzer Prizes. John Updike signed my book *Good luck, John Updike.*

MY FATHER CONDUCTS
MAHLER'S NINTH

At Radio Shack, I leave my father with Jeremy, our kindest salesperson of the day. "How can you buy what you don't try?" I hear my father say. A plastic grocery bag hangs from his fingers. Inside the bag, a long-playing record, Mahler's Ninth. After my mother died last month, my father started shopping for turntables. I stare at plasma TVs, where Shrek eyes me into infinity.

"Customer service," my father says later, as we pull out of the parking lot. "Just words." He makes a clicking noise with his tongue, the same noise he makes when solving crossword puzzles, the squares blank, refusing his plans.

"But you can't expect them to let you—" I say, before my father waves his hand.

"*There's* your problem," he says.

In Circuit City the employees wear red vests and black pants. My father talks with Brittany, who's embarrassed by this embarrassing man with his embarrassing bag. "I can like, ask a manager or something if you want or?" Brittany says. Before my father can answer, a telephone summons Brittany, who answers it like she's won a prize. "It's getting so that you can just *disappear*," my father whispers. We leave down an aisle of Shreks injecting their good-natured grumpiness into the world.

Best Buy is even worse, with a kid who seems twelve years old working the audio/visual section. From a tower of TVs, a hundred Shreks admonish a hundred silly donkeys.

"Is Shrek on every TV in the universe?" I say.

"Yeah!" the kid says, brightly, but his mood is broken when my father unpacks the record and asks if he can try it out. "To test," he says. My father invites the kid to hold the record, which he does. "What's this supposed to be?" the kid asks.

In the car my father presses the lighter in and out, in and out.

"I wish you wouldn't do that," I say.

My father stares ahead, where it has just begun to snow. "Who is this Shrek?" he says.

I drive to the local college. I tell my father we can find some vinyl stores around here. We do, but none that sell turntables. "You can try Goodwill," an employee named Chloe tells us. Chloe owns three turntables, she says. "But turntables are like, super-valuable. For deejaying and whatever."

"We are not deejays," my father says.

"Really?" Chloe says.

In Goodwill the air smells of damp wool and cardboard. "I kind of liked Chloe," I say. My father doesn't hear. We find the stereo equipment at the back of the store, pricier than you'd imagine. We find a rack system with a turntable. My father unsheathes the record and places it on the platter.

"It won't work," I say.

But I'm wrong. The record spins. The tone arm rises. My father closes his eyes and raises his hand, as if to conduct.

"These never work," I say.

"Shh," my father says, "it's starting."

COLLECTING

They both collected things, without really knowing it. He collected leaves, old bills, grocery bags, and coins. She collected low-fat
cookbooks, fashion magazines, water bottles, and soup labels (there were
coupons on them, also collected). He collected shells whenever the two
of them went to the beach, sometimes with the friends she managed to
collect at work. They were nice enough, he guessed, although he preferred
going to the beach with Flashy, the dog they'd recently purchased from
a local pet shelter, whose collection had overgrown. They both liked to
take Flashy on long walks: he loved fetching sticks, saliva collecting at the
corners of his mouth. They walked to the park, where sunlight collected
atop the duck pond, enjoying the stares of babies, who peered from stroll-
ers while their parents collected their picnic blankets, plastic spoons, and
paper plates.

Sometimes she got angry with him about his coins. Why did he insist
upon collecting them in the coffee mug she'd gotten him on their first
trip to beach together? Why did he place the mug on top of the refrigerator, where it rattled when the compressor kicked in, and where he never
remembered to clean, dust and grime collecting along the freezer's edge?
The coins were mostly pennies anyway (she'd used the quarters for parking meters, although she'd collected two tickets in the past month), whose
collective total was probably less than two dollars. Two dollars—the mug
had cost thirteen! She felt a gray sort of anger collecting inside her, like

the dryer lint he could never remember to clean, collecting there, for her to scrape away.

For his part, he wished she would stop inviting coworkers to the beach. Sometimes, on the drive home, he felt himself about to say something, but instead collected his thoughts, which tended to wander, especially when they crossed the peninsula bridge, which summoned his fear of heights, collected from years of cross-country travel (his father lived out west, where he collected unemployment). Why the need for coworkers? Wasn't his companionship enough? Wasn't *he* enough? He'd said this once, to Flashy, when he was removing the briars and sea grass that'd collected beneath his fur. But Flashy had only licked his paws, lost in dog recollection.

One evening, they had an argument. They said things they'd both later regret. He grabbed Flashy and drove to the beach; she stayed at home and tried to collect herself. When night approached and she still hadn't heard from him, she began to worry. It was nearly dark when the telephone rang.

"It's me," he said. "Listen, I locked my keys and wallet and cell phone and Flashy in the car—"

"You locked Flashy in the car?" she said.

"Excuse me, sir," an operator's voice interrupted. "But how would you like to pay for the call?"

WASH THEORY

Plates, large:
Stack in bottom row. Front side should face the rinse cylinder. Do not face plates away from the rinse cylinder. Do not stack in top row. If washing by hand, make sure to wash both sides evenly and with equal care. It cannot be stated enough: a plate has *two sides*.

Glasses:
Always stack in top row, even if you have space available below. Remember: a bottom-stacked glass is a broken glass. Glasses may be hand-washed, but must be never be towel-dried, especially wine glasses and champagne flutes. A towel-dried champagne flute is the last word in amateurism. DON'T DO THIS!

Coffee mugs:
Top row stacking is preferable, but coffee mugs may, in rare instances, be placed in the bottom row, if room permits. Hand rinse all mugs before stacking. Use Scrubee or hard sponge for all sugar/coffee residues. Remember, as in all other matters of washing: you do the *work*—the machine *finishes*.

Plates, small:
Rinse cold, stack in bottom row or top, if space available. Advanced: a small plate may be successfully wedged into the bottom row, perpendic-

ular to the silverware holder, provided that the plate does not block the rinse jets. If plate clinks during spray cycle, discontinue bottom wedging.

Silverware:
Silverware technique is largely a matter of personal taste, but it should be noted that no single technique satisfies all silverware needs—be willing to experiment. In general, silverware should be loaded "bouquet" style, with ends up to ensure maximum rinsing; however, in some instances, silverware may be placed handles up, as in the case of steak knives and serving spoons. Wooden-handled knives should never be machine washed, even if manufacturer's silverware holder has a separate wash column for such purposes. Silverware is silverware; wood is wood. Confusion can only breed confusion.

On drying racks:
A well-stacked drying rack builds naturally and organically from a well-defined center. Do not use pre-assigned drying slots, or, in lieu of rack, stack wet dishes on a towel. Remember: your washing is a reflection of *you*. Save large bowls, pots and pans for last, as these may successfully "dome" a carefully organized drying rack. Advanced: hang measuring cups from ends of salad tongs.

"Fringe" items:
Colanders should always be hand-washed as should all salad bowls and cooking utensils. A whisk should be washed as silverware (above). Mushroom brushes defy washing, and should be avoided, if possible. A cheese grater may be soaked in soapy water, but should not be left to soak overnight, or re-soaked before washing. A good theory never equates soaking and washing.

Competing Theory:
Leave dishes in sink until tomorrow. Someone else will wash them. Someone always does.

HORN LESSONS, 1980

My horn, a student model, rarely left its case, which was furred with carpet and gave off a whiff of valve oil and fruit roll-ups. The mouthpiece could be stored behind a small panel; removing it a kind of expected thrill, like finding a dollar in your church jacket. The mouthpiece was funnel-shaped and could be sounded without the horn, as our bus rides home often proved, the car unlucky enough to pull close behind us serenaded by Michael DiMano buzzing *Honk if you like my schlongus* or Darren Giles intoning *Your tits—for President!*

My music teacher, Mr. Philips, often spent entire lessons swapping knock-knock jokes with me. One of his favorites was *Knock-knock. Who's There? Banana. Banana who? Banana split, so ice creamed!* When the lesson was nearly over, he'd ask me to play the assigned exercise. I'd hold the horn to my lips, rest the bell to my leg, and blindly spurt the idea of the first few measures until I'd somehow reached the end, when Mr. Philips would break the silence between us by saying, "Well, certainly no fear of notes here."

Once I left the horn in my father's trunk when he drove to Virginia Beach, returning, a week later, with a different car.

Another time I'd rolled a nickel into its center and had to flush the tubing with a clothes hanger.

The week before Thanksgiving I dropped the horn into a snow bank and left it there until I'd finished sledding.

But more often I did nothing with horn, surprising myself by opening the case and taking in the horn's beauty as if for the first time, which it almost was. I'd prank my friends by putting the phone receiver into the horn, then blowing so hard my eyes watered.

This is all to say that I greeted playing Mozart's Horn Concerto Number 1, K412, with some trepidation.

The night of the concert I wore a white sportcoat. The gym floor was waxy, newly polished. The basketball backboards, firm as the sun and moon in my mind, had been drawn up into the rafters. The concert began. Mr. Philips shot me a hopeful look. What can I say? I lifted the horn and played. My parents were in the audience. I remember applause, a feeling of relief. There is a photograph of me from that night, standing on the podium with Mr. Philips. He has his hand on my shoulder, the horn tucked under my arm. If you look closely you can see my fingers gripping the underside of the bell. You can see the whiteness of my knuckles.

So have many of my enterprises begun, with a firm grasp of what I've never known.

NOT STUART

Not Stuart—*please.*

We want Phoebe, beautiful Phoebe, with her mouth parted like a halved plum—that was *going* to be a line—who has now overslept her alarm, leaving Stuart, her husband, to slip from the bed and become the sudden understudy of this story. Admittedly, I must shoulder some of the blame: I had forgotten about Stuart. He'd gone out drinking the night before, stumbling home, then passing out in bed alongside Phoebe, his wife of ten years, who, on the morning of our interruption, was finally going to leave Stuart for good, stealing away with a family of Jehovah's Witnesses. It was going to be wonderful, I swear.

But now gone, all of that. Farewell Phoebe, with her milky (I'd deleted *alabaster*) hands and delicate fingers. *She* was the one we wanted, full of poetry and woe, but now she has rolled onto her side, as Stuart wakes. He sits on the side of the bed, picking beneath his toenails with Phoebe's brass letter opener.

Stuart, I'm begging you, turn around, go back to bed—please!

But does he listen? (This is one of the many reasons Phoebe was going to leave him, by the way, his *inability to listen*, especially when he was watching basketball with his feet on the coffee table.) Instead, Stuart makes his way downstairs, where he's surprised to discover a clean mixing bowl, wooden spoon, and box of pancake mix sitting on the kitchen countertop. I had left these items for Phoebe, on this, the morning of her emancipation (she was *supposed* to have an epiphany while mixing the batter) before her departure with the Jehovah's Witnesses, but, like everything else this morning ... well, let's not talk about it.

Stuart reads the cooking instructions, and then walks to the pantry, where he removes a box of raisins. He studies the front picture for what seems to me too long a time, then raises the box to his mouth and pours in an avalanche of sweet, sticky raisins.

Upstairs, not much can be said for Phoebe. She is still sleeping, hair splayed across the pillow, eyes closed. It is in these moments that I wonder how she ever chose poor Stuart as a husband (I hadn't really thought this through, I now realize), but we may suppose it was the usual mix of pity and hope that is the bringer of so many marriages. Anyway, I must report—regretfully—that I now see something I hadn't noticed before: a thin string of drool hanging from the corner of Phoebe's mouth.

Let's return to Stuart, who has spent the past few minutes trying to decide if raisins go with pancakes. He's familiar with banana and blueberry (Phoebe used to make these for him when they were first married) but raisin, what about raisin? he wonders. He looks at the box, skeptically, then raises it again to his mouth and wriggles his tongue inside. At the exact moment when he stretches his tongue to its fullest extent (he has a repulsively large tongue) he hears the double chime of the doorbell, and turns toward the front door.

Through the front window, partially obscured by a thin curtain, Stuart can see two Jehovah's Witnesses.

As I mentioned, the Witnesses were supposed to be for Phoebe. I won't bore you with all the details, but there was going to be a wonderful line where one of them asked Phoebe, "Have you been crying, dear?" to which Phoebe, who has just decided to leave Stuart, replied, "I've been crying my whole life."

Well, forget all that. Stuart, who has made two perfectly sweet telemarketers cry in the past month, approaches the front door. He parts the curtain with one hand. The Witnesses smile, say hello. Stuart looks at them for a moment and then opens his mouth, wide, revealing a brown tongue-heap of fresh raisin goo. Stuart!

The Witnesses leave with their arms around each other.

I have to admit that I'm a little impressed with Stuart's response. In retrospect, my "I've been crying my whole life" seems sentimental. So, I think it only fair to grudgingly score Stuart one point. (Stuart: 1, Me: 0.)

Phoebe, who was already falling out of our favor the last time we checked in, is still sleeping upstairs, a dark, damp circle of drool the size of a quarter beneath her parted mouth. I'm beginning to wonder why I was so fascinated with that mouth in the first place, really. I can now see tiny cracks around the left corner of her lip that I hadn't noticed before.

Stuart, pleased with his performance, heads into the bathroom to blow his nose. He takes two tissues at a time from the box, blows, then tosses them towards the trash can, imagining a three-second clock ticking down inside him, the last shot of a basketball game. When he misses, Stuart shoots again from a closer distance.

It has now occurred to me that some characters have behaved horribly during the course of this story (I won't even bother discussing what we just saw in the bathroom). I think I may have made an error in judgment this time around: do Phoebe and Stuart deserve to have their story told? Let me submit, also, some new, disturbing information I discovered while Stuart was leading his team to victory.

Finding myself bored with Stuart's shenanigans, I wandered upstairs again to check on Phoebe, and was shocked to see her sitting upright, knees drawn up into her chest. I watched her as she listened to Stuart. When Stuart headed upstairs again, Phoebe slid back under the sheets and closed her eyes.

Could it be that Phoebe, my chosen one, was never really asleep this whole time? Could it be that she watched Stuart as he rose from bed and walked downstairs? Could it be that I've been fooled this whole time, arranging a world for Phoebe, when she wanted absolutely nothing to do with it?

Phoebe!

YARD WORK

For the past few weeks my neighbor has been trimming his yard with scissors. He usually starts in the evening, when I've just finished putting my son to bed and my wife is watching reality TV with the volume off. I can see him outside, crouched to the lawn, his hands working furiously. His expression is neither happy nor sad. Sometimes he wears a baseball cap, sometimes not. I don't know his name.

On the show my wife mutely watches, a group of college kids have been tasked with circumnavigating the world in a school bus. They seem angry about this. They are always angry. They yell and scream things we'll never know. Sometimes they hang glide or visit landmarks. Stonehenge, for example.

At first I thought my neighbor was using a weeding tool. One of those things that looks like a giant fork—that thing. But it wasn't that thing; it was scissors. I saw them when I went to the end of my driveway under the pretense of taking the trash out. I waved to my neighbor and he waved back with the scissors. I left the empty trashcan at the end of the driveway and came back inside where my son was out of bed, watching the reality show with my wife. We've been working on getting him to stop doing that, along with brushing his top row of teeth, not just the bottom, the way he always does.

My neighbor has been working on the grass around his mailbox for nearly three days now. After that, he'll move on to grass along the walkway. That seems like his plan, if he has one. You'd figure a guy cutting his lawn with scissors would have some kind of plan.

Tonight I have to read my son another bedtime story, to get him back to sleep. We keep getting him different books from the library, but they all seem to deliver the same news: *the world is more exciting than you'll ever know—now go to sleep.* Most times I don't think my son is even paying attention. He gets this look on his face.

Later I drink a beer I don't really want and watch my neighbor finish the grass around the mailbox. I watch him from my living room window. My wife watches TV. It gets dark out. My neighbor scoops scissored grass into a black garbage bag. He fills the bag, then another. I think he should be ready to start on the grass along the walkway, but he doesn't. What he does is cross the street and start on my yard. He cuts my grass.

"Come look," I whisper to my wife.

But she's already left the room.

In the morning, bags line the curb, knotted with yellow ties.

FALLING OUTS

Mary Stephenson and Renee Ward no longer speak to one another, although you may remember them as co-editors of the student yearbook, although each served as the other's maid of honor, although each is the mother of two boys who once played in each other's backyards while Mary and Renee drank cranberry tonics from a glass pitcher dewed with moisture, the boys' play marking the silence between them; Mary's attention, Renee noticed, wandering to her gold wristwatch, a gift, she supposed, from Phil, whom Renee had once tried to dissuade Mary from marrying, a conversation they never brought up again, although Mary always felt that was the beginning of the end between them.

John Stokes and Brandon Sims no longer drink beer in the parking lot, no longer swap mixed tapes, no longer have semi-philosophical conversations about the phoniness of it all, no longer wear their shirt collars up, no longer privately wonder whether there might be something vaguely homosexual between them, and no longer feel any need to know the other's thoughts, feelings, hopes, dreams, fears, worries, or whereabouts.

Joanne Gray, Max Andresani, and Tyler Hughes have not cut class together in years and cannot imagine whatever it was that drove them to do so all those times, Joanne driving them to McDonalds in her father's BMW, a car that afforded Tyler a sudden glimpse of his future, pointing him toward law school when his head had only been hitherto filled with drums, he and Max two-thirds of a ska band, *Sound Advice*, whose performance at the senior talent show survives in no-one's memory and was later erased by Max's mother, Freda, to record the opening ceremonies of the 1996 Summer Olympics.

Janet Greiner and Ashley Clayton have not had anything to say to one another in years, having once exchanged hugs outside Superfresh, where each was too busy thinking how awful the other looked to notice how little the two of them had actually changed since high school, where they had always thought the other looked awful.

Jeremy Giles and Scott Cooper have no desire to perform *Saturday Night Live* sketches in the senior lounge, have no idea why so many yearbook photos were taken of them doing so, and have both lied, on several occasions about the whereabouts of their yearbooks, both to their wives and even, in Scott's case, his eldest daughter, Sophia, whose mother put her up to it.

John Orr and Heather Wilkinson, having fallen out before everyone else, having become "sworn enemies" after John, terrified by his secret and mystifying attraction to Heather, called out, "Hey, why don't you ride *my* bike?" to Heather as she clumsily pedaled by his bus on her rickety Schwinn, have since fallen in love, married, and raised three beautiful children together. John works for DuPont; Heather for Bank of America. They live in Delaware.

THE DIARY

When Francine got a diary for her tenth birthday, she wrote late into the night, while her mother slept and her brother did whatever it was her brother did. *He likes to watch TV and eat peanut butter off a fork*, Francine wrote, but that didn't seem to capture her brother at all. *He has brown hair and brown eyes*, she wrote, but that, too, didn't seem right. One time she had caught Robert praying to the stereo, on which a record turned. Robert had his eyes closed, hands together, ears muffed with headphones. For a moment he lifted a hand to the turntable like he was blessing it. Francine watched him until he seemed like someone she did not truly know. A stranger. *Robert likes music*, Francine wrote.

Francine's mother worked at a travel agency. Sometimes Francine took the school bus to her office and waited around until she was ready to drive her home. She liked waiting around the office, which had a water cooler that sent air bubbles to the surface when you filled your cup. Francine thought the bubbles looked like jellyfish. *My mom is the biggest spaz!* Francine wrote, the night of one of these visits. *She won't even let me wear fake earrings!* That evening the two of them had stopped for dinner at Howard Johnson's where her mother had started crying during dessert.

"Mom, what's wrong?" Francine asked, but her mother waved a hand and said it was nothing, nothing at all.

"I was thinking of the time we all stopped at a Howard Johnson's on our drive out east. Do you remember? That seems like such a long time ago." Later, they drove home in silence. *Pierced ears aren't even a big deal anymore*, Francine wrote. *They're like, normal.*

At school, one of Francine's classmates locked herself in the princi-pal's car and refused to come out until her father showed up. The two of them sat in the car a while, talking. Francine watched them from her bus window, on which someone had written WASH ME. She found herself feeling both superior to and jealous of the girl—how was this possible? *Our bus is really gross*, Francine wrote. *It smells like feet.*

One weekend, Francine spent the night at her friend Allison's house. Allison's mom let them stay up as late as they wished, watching TV, eating snacks. "You girls just enjoy being the wonderful girls you are," Allison's mom said, and Allison said, "Mom, you sound so *gay* saying that."

"Well, if gay means happy, then I guess I'm gay," Allison's mom said. "I'm very, very, very gay." Later, Allison cried. "She's *drunk*," she said. "Oh, please don't ever tell anyone, *please*."

That night, Francine couldn't think of anything to write in the diary. She listened to Allison snoring beside her. She couldn't sleep. Years later, after the diary had long since vanished, Francine still could still recall staying up all night. How she'd been afraid. How she'd wanted to wake Allison, but couldn't.

HE DIDN'T WANT TO TALK ABOUT IT

You could ask him, but he didn't want to talk about it. He'd give you this look if you asked him about it. Like you'd just asked him for a million dollars, which you hadn't; you'd just asked him about it. That's all. But he didn't want to talk about it, the way he never wanted to talk about it. He'd look out the window. He'd order another drink. He'd say, "What happened to your hair?" when he knew very well nothing had happened to your hair—he was only trying not to talk about it, even after you'd said nothing had happened to your hair. What did he mean?

"I just thought something happened to it," he'd say. Like that explained something. But if you asked him what he meant, suddenly he didn't want to talk about it.

He didn't want to talk about it in the morning, when he was straightening his tie in the bathroom mirror, or on the weekends, when he liked to eat eggs and watch basketball. He didn't want to talk about it on holidays or vacations or trips to the lumber store, where he always spent the longest time, looking. It was crazy how long he spent at the lumber store, looking, but if you pointed this out, it just became something else he didn't want to talk about, and then where were you? Back to asking him about it and him not wanting to talk about it. Where else?

You could think of ways to ask him about it without appearing to be asking about it, but he'd know what you were up to. He'd make the face he always made when you were asking him about something but really trying to ask about it, when he'd made it clear, so abundantly clear in so many ways that he didn't want to talk about it, not now, not ever, world without end, amen. What would it take it for him to make you understand that he didn't want to talk about it?

You could try not thinking about it. Maybe if you stopped thinking about it, you wouldn't think to ask him about it, and then he wouldn't have to not want to talk about it, but this never worked, for as soon as you thought about not thinking about it, there you were thinking about it—it, it, *it!*—until you found yourself asking him about it again. Why wouldn't he talk about it, even just a little? Maybe you'd stop asking, if he talked about it just a little. Couldn't he see how talking about it a little would stop you from asking about it? Certainly he had to see that.

He did, he said. But he didn't want to talk about it.

WHAT I WOULD TELL THE SQUIRRELS

You're scarier than you think. Use it; own it.

Love that little forward/backwards thing you do underneath moving automobiles—super!

Small suggestion: it might be nice to rid the world of snakes (they've been saying stuff about you, in case you were wondering).

Acorns are gross.

Kudos to spreading your squirrel empire across the globe!

Sometimes I'll see one of you scampering across the yard and realize I'm not even registering you scampering across the yard, the way you craftily assert your non-presence in my life, over and over again, like milk or taillights.

You're not going to supplant the rabbits. The rabbits are here to stay.

It's not so much that we don't want you in the attic as that we don't want you feeling like the attic is "yours." Capische?

Those tails are amazing! I mean, just *wow*.

Let the other squirrel have the acorn, every once in a while.

I can tell when you're dreaming.

The way I envision you harming me goes something like this: you're trapped in the garage when I appear holding a kitchen broom and trash-can lid. I approach, only wishing to problem solve when—your squirrel teeth upon my neck!

You could do with less skittishness.

"Rosebud" is Charles Foster Kane's sled.

Your considerable knowledge of trees and telephone poles is both admirable and astounding, and something, quite frankly, a dolphin would have a difficult time mastering.

Enough already with the chattering.

Look left, right, and *then left again.*

For nearly seven years I had no idea how to insert page numbers in Microsoft Word and lived in constant fear that someone would ask me to do so.

Be yourself.

You are sleek, agile, and fleet. I've always been a little in awe of you.

Nobody likes a tagalong.

THE INTERSECTION

On the way to the dinner theatre, Robbie's father rolled the window down for a woman crying at an intersection. The woman wore a heavy coat and the kind of gloves Robbie had seen only in photographs of Jackie Kennedy. She was sitting on the median with her hands to her face. The coat was missing a sleeve. The woman's hair was wild, windblown.

"Excuse me," Robbie's father said, "but do you need some help?"

The woman looked at him like he'd interrupted a phone call. "Do you know what I need?" she said. "I need someone to tell me I'm beautiful sometimes." Her words were thick and incorrect. "*That's* what I need."

"Jim," Robbie's mother said, "the light's turning green."

"I need someone to be honest with me, just for once," the woman said.

"Jim, the light."

Robbie could see a scar along the woman's jaw. Pink and smooth as a seashell's lining.

"I need someone to call me honey." She ran a hand through her hair. "You know what I mean?"

His father's neck tensed the way it did when he pulled the bag from the kitchen trash. He faced forward, as if the woman wasn't speaking at all.

"I don't think it's too much to ask," she said. "Do you?"

When they pulled away, Robbie could see the woman watching him. He ducked out of view, wondering if she would show up at the theatre and pull him from his chair.

"The poor woman," Robbie's mother whispered.

"Hmph," his father said. He made a gesture that Robbie's mother disapproved of. "Oh, you're bad," she said. But she laughed anyway.

The theatre was dark, crowded. Robbie and his parents ate their food as an actor took the stage, singing a song about the problems women bring. In the dark, the people around Robbie seemed both distant and near. He could just make out his parents' faces, his father's embarrassing smile, his mother's pale chin. Robbie heard them laugh, but the laughter was like something he was no longer a part of.

"Mom, Dad," he said.

When they turned, their expressions informed Robbie that he had begun to cry.

"Sometimes I think about what would happen if you two died," he said. "And it's like I just don't know what I would do."

DUMMY

I like to sleep in cars. Especially with the windows down and a song on the radio. Once, I spent an entire drive from Boston to Washington DC beneath a wool blanket. A woman who would become my first wife was driving; her sister, who had once survived a plane crash and was then dying of cancer, rode in the passenger seat. Cancer and a plane crash—the odds! The blanket was green, flecked with dog hair and pine needles. A Christmas tree must have once ridden back here, I thought. Tough job, getting it through the back door.

We went to the National Gallery, the day I slept beneath the blanket. I remember snow, slush, me following the two women, feeling both happy and vaguely left out, all the while, too, a sense of still being underneath the blanket. I could feel it around my shoulders. I remember drinking from a fountain, afraid I'd accidentally get it wet.

When her sister died, my wife took up guitar. Once I found her playing along to a Stones album I'd forgotten we had. She was in the living room, where I like to go at night and lie beneath a blanket, watching ESPN with the volume off. I like doing that sometimes. She had her eyes closed, strumming along to the music, although you couldn't hear her at all. I watched her for a while, the tension in her fingers, lips.

They weren't close sisters. They'd fought. They'd said things they'd both later regret. My wife's sister was a slow learner, the family said. Dummy, my sister had called her. *Dummy.* One time they'd gone to a football game and my wife had refused to sit with her, her dummy sister, so she'd sat on the visitor's side, shunning this dummy. But Dummy missed her, couldn't follow the game, lost her jacket in the jaws of the bleachers. Wept. A neighbor heard her crying out to my sister, across the field, too far to hear. "What's the point?" she'd cried, meaning the score. "Oh, what's the point?"

CAN OPENER VS. MAHLER'S FIFTH

CAN OPENER: Can be machine-washed or hand-washed.

MAHLER'S FIFTH: Opens with a Death March.

CAN OPENER: We've had the same one for years, green-handled, kept in a drawer beneath the microwave.

MAHLER'S FIFTH: Premiered in 1904, Mahler conducting.

CAN OPENER: Surprisingly heavy. Sometimes used to tap dents into the lids of vacuum-sealed jars. Pickles, especially.

MAHLER'S FIFTH: Mahler's wife, Alma, disliked it, and told her husband so. Mahler nodded. Made changes.

CAN OPENER: No one is really sure what to call the little circular cutter, the sharp wheel that pierces the can and always seems a bit rusty no matter how many times you wash it. The saw? The blade?

MAHLER'S FIFTH: Leonard Bernstein said he wished to be buried with the score.

CAN OPENER: I once used it to win an argument, or so it seemed to me. It was Christmas and I was standing by the kitchen sink, opening a can of something, I don't remember. What I remember is saying, "You've said that every Christmas for the past six years," punctuating each word with a turn of the handle.

MAHLER'S FIFTH: Composed in a summer cottage. Mahler took long swims in the morning. The lake dusted with pollen.

CAN OPENER: Essential for opening certain brands of cat food. Fancy Feast, for example.

MAHLER'S FIFTH: Several different versions of the score exist, a source of debate for scholars, musicians.

CAN OPENER: Favorite use will always be opening slender cans of mandarin oranges. The way the juice clings to them, even as you lift one to your lips.

MAHLER'S FIFTH: Upon hearing the first performance, Mahler lingered backstage, idly twisting a white handkerchief between his fingers. Chairs were stacked against the wall. The air smelled of valve oil and gas lamps.

CAN OPENER: Has outlived three toaster ovens, two cats, and three cars. The last a Honda Civic with 181, 777 miles. Transmission. What can you do?

MAHLER'S FIFTH: In a moment, he knew, he would have to greet his wife. She would say something encouraging, the way she always did, not wanting to hurt him. Their marriage was slipping away. How had that happened? He knew he'd have to say something, but it wasn't until he saw her, readying her praise, that he knew what it was. *Nobody understood it.*

SLEEP

The kind he had as a boy, heavier, it seems to him now, than what passes between his nightly routine of classical radio and waking to a comforter balled between his feet. What happened to that kind of sleep? The sense of it, arching over his bedroom like a tent, whose folds tapered to a point he ascended to each night when the only sound was his father turning off the hallway light, the bright band beneath his door disappearing, vanished. He'd dreamt of flat lawns, stretching into forever. He'd dreamt of reading books whose pages had forgotten their words.

But sleep was not easy. He'd had to renew its idea by moving his hands beneath the pillow, seeking the cool places not yet warmed by his fingers. Sometimes he feared that someone was watching him and he'd find himself snapping his nightstand lamp on, *aha*, only to be greeted by the sight of his room, daytime dull, ordinary as an undershirt. Summer nights, his electric fan asked him a question, then turned its head, snubbing him. Hidden pipes sighed behind the walls. He'd rolled to one side, listening.

But he'd slept in other places, too, and hadn't that been another kind of sleep? He'd slept in sleeping bags on hard floors, floors of friends, church groups, the bag's interior lined like a mitten and smelling faintly of milk, hair, and clapped erasers. He'd slept in his grandparent's guest room, which confused sleep with its incorrect nightstand, upon which a round clock wore two bright bells like earmuffs. He'd slept on his mother's coat during *The Nutcracker*. What about the sleep that found him in the back seat of station wagons, his sister's feet troubling his, requiring kicking, or the sleep that arrived on airplanes, following him into the sky? What kind of sleep greeted him in his hospital crib?

In kindergarten, his class had been made to put their heads down during naptime. These moments, recalled now, seem to him the rarest kind of sleep. For he'd always been awake, as had everyone else, their heads to their desks, looking into each other's faces, suppressing laughter. Their teacher would join them in this routine, pretending to sleep. "Shh," she'd say, if anyone giggled. "We're sleeping."

The children would watch each other, waiting. Then someone would close their eyes, and then another and another, until there was nothing left to do but close your own, thinking, *I will.*

MY FAMILY RECALLS A COOKOUT,
CIRCA 1989

MOM: We took a picture of you kids in the pool. You're wearing a snorkel. Uncle Rick is throwing Amanda into the deep end. If you look close you can see Uncle Rick's can of beer on the diving board. Rolling Rock.

DAD: We ate those turkey burgers or chicken burgers or whatever the hell they were. I chucked mine in the hydrangea bushes when Amanda was screaming at Rick. She was so mad. Remember? I didn't know she knew all those words, but she did. Boy, she knew them all right.

SISTER: Uncle Rick was a mental case, if you ask me. The way he kept pretending the hot dogs were screaming when he put them on the grill? That seemed weird to me. That plus the cops taking him away.

ME: All I remember is being really scared of Uncle Rick, too. The way he kept talking in a phony British accent for no reason. *Care for a spot of tea-ay?*

UNCLE RICK: I think I've grown both mentally and spiritually since then. That was a low time for me. I can admit that now. That's not something I'm ashamed to admit. As my sponsor always says, Admit to what needs admitting; do what is before you to do.

SISTER: I guess it all started with the Rolling Rock cans. Uncle Rick kept doing this thing where he'd stand on the diving board and toss each empty can high into the air. When they landed in the pool, Uncle Rick would pretend to shoot them with an "air musket." That's what he told me he was doing anyway. Shooting those cans with an air musket.

DAD: I don't know why we couldn't just have normal hamburgers. That's what I told your mother. I said, Why couldn't we just have normal hamburgers? She said, This is what Amanda likes. I said, Since when? She said, Since you can have a hot dog. I said, I like a little hamburger with my hot dog, thank you very much, but she didn't say anything. I'd still waiting for an answer. Why couldn't we just have normal hamburgers?

ME: I didn't even realize Uncle Rick had thrown Amanda into the pool. It happened so fast. All I heard was her shrieking. And then the splash. It was a really big splash. Huge.

MOM: You kids always loved being in the pool with Uncle Rick when you were little. He was such a zany uncle! *Uncle Rick, Uncle Rick!* you'd say, and then Uncle Rick would put you on his shoulders and carry you to the deep end, where he'd do that funny thing like he was drowning and you two would scream, *Help! Mom! Dad! Help!* and then Uncle Rick would surface beneath your legs and launch you into the shallow end. Remember? I think your uncle didn't realize how much you'd grown up since then. Those kinds of games really weren't your thing anymore. But he didn't know.

SISTER: So I said, Hey, Uncle Rick, don't be a litterbug! and the next thing I know Uncle Rick picked me up like he was going to throw me into the pool. But I wasn't wearing my bathing suit. I was wearing my new pair of Gap jeans—my first ever pair of Gap jeans—and that asymmetrical top from The Limited since I wasn't even planning on staying at the cookout; I was planning on going to the mall with Darcy Greenblatt.

UNCLE RICK: I've been fortunate to start life anew here in beautiful New Hampshire. It's early fall now, the leaves just starting to turn, the air redolent of wood smoke. I enjoy evening walks this time of year, especially when the light has just begun to fade and tree branches sway gently in the breeze. Yesterday I discovered a dobsonfly in the hatchery.

ME: When the cops showed up, I remember Dad telling them it was all a misunderstanding, just a little family horseplay, that's all. But the cops said they'd received a complaint. They came into the patio area and had a talk with Uncle Rick. They were both really young looking, I remember. They wore these crazy shiny shoes. I remember thinking how weird those shoes looked.

SISTER: And then he carried me to end of the diving board and threw me. "Tally-Ho!" he cried in that stupid accent. His idea was, he later explained to Mom, that I was a hound out to hunt those foxy cans.

DAD: I always figure a neighbor made the call, what with Amanda's screaming and everything. She really was a little out of control. But those cops didn't need to take Rick inside their cruiser and fingerprint him. Totally unnecessary. Waste of taxpayer dollars.

ME: Amanda really could scream when she wanted to. I'll never forget the way she screamed that day. Never.

UNCLE RICK: *Sitting quietly, doing nothing; spring comes, and the grass grows by itself.*

MOM: I still think it's a nice picture. Maybe not perfect, but nice. If only Amanda had remembered to smile!

WHAT A NIGHT SKY

For the moment, they stand. All three of them, two fathers from two unfinished stories and the boy, whose name is still not known. Zeke? Not Zeke. Please. Leave it as "the boy" and come back to it later. It won't be clear for a while, like the weather, which has deposited these three at the door, knocking, looking for shelter. It is raining, and none of them quite understand why they are here, three strangers before a strange house, with the wind at their backs. (A terrible beginning.)

What is clear, however, is that the boy will star in this story while the fathers get the short end of the stick. The fathers feel resigned to this. Already the two of them have formed a loose sort of kinship, the first (Father A?) offering a cigarette to Father B, who, although he does not smoke, accepts and takes a seat alongside Father A, who has graciously swept a twig from the porch and offered the (dry) tail of his trench coat as a cushion. They smoke without speaking. It does not surprise them when the rain inexplicably turns to snow and begins blowing in on them. They turn their coat collars up (they have identical coats) and wait it out. Snow catches in their eyelashes. They do not brush it away. It does not surprise them when the boy gives an astonished gasp, and exclaims, "I have the key!"

He does. It's been in his pocket the whole time. He discovered it back when the men were first knocking on the door, which accounts for the cartoonish expression he turns on them now, dangling the shiny key like a prize fish. It is his way to delight in things like that—the hidden detail—

even though both fathers' shoes are now dusted with snow and Father A's toes are nearly numb.

The boy unlocks the door, and enters the house. Father A gives Father B a look. Father B recognizes the look, not only because he is more intuitive than he himself imagines, but also because he and Father A have nearly identical facial features, which is sort of nice. Father A holds the door for Father B. Father B mumbles thanks and passes inside.

What The Boy Sees
Light. Fantastic light pouring in through tall, curtain-less windows. A cathedral, he thinks. Put that in. A holy place. Put in the feeling of the house at Christmas, with the tree in the living room reflecting light against the sliding glass doors. Put in the feeling of taking decorations from the box and arranging them around the lights, all the while imagining that someone—the President, say—was watching, amazed. Don't forget the feeling of crawling beneath the tree, either, when you could hear the lights blinking within their casing and you thought about living the rest of your life inside a Christmas tree. That's the kind of house this is. A holy house. A house of light.

What Father B Sees
A recliner covered with a white slipcloth (you couldn't say "slipcover" without repeating "cover"). It's got wide rounded arms and a generous seat cushion. A good, solid piece of furniture. Father B tests it with his fingers, then sits on the edge of the cushion, not wanting to disrupt the smoothness of its wrapping. Someone (the owner?) has taken great care to make sure that every inch has been accounted for; an idea that pleases Father B. He runs his hand along the arms, feeling a kind of satisfaction in the tightness of the cloth, its texture, strength. He is surprised to find himself moved by this. He did not know, until now, that he cared for such things. Father B has only been inside the house for a few minutes now, but already he feels much wiser than the character who sat outside and smoked a cigarette with Father A. For example, it occurs to him now that he is quiet and circumspect, a lover of golf and newspapers, happy in a roundabout way. He does not *want*, which explains, in part, why his story has gone unfinished. There is no room for him in fiction, although

he does not know this. Unaware of a world that cares little for him, he eases back into the recliner and begins his fabulous exile. And his mood is broken only slightly when he observes Father A pulling the covers off all the other furniture.

What Father A Sees

What is this? And *this*? Such incredible things! Father A gathers the covers into his arms, heart pounding. So poorly imagined is Father A that the only objects he previously understood were his cigarettes and trench coat. The rain terrified him. The snow made the things underneath his trench coat ache. He wanted to ask Father B about it, but whenever he looked at Father B a strange feeling passed through him and left him speechless. Father A does not know, and will never know, that he and Father B share the same consciousness, although Father B is warming up to the idea. He stands beside Father A now and helps him with the covers. "A chair," he explains. "A table." "A picture frame." "An oyster spoon."

"An oyster spoon," Father A says, dreamily.

"My name is Richard," Father B says.

"Richard."

"And yours is 'Robert.'"

Upstairs

More light! The boy runs to the windows and throws open the curtains. It is night now, and fat stars hang in the sky like—but who can describe the stars? The boy knows several things the others do not: 1) he must open windows because a description of the breeze will be the penultimate line of this story, 2) Richard will rest his arms upon the sill, 3) Robert will be at another window, taking in his first view of stars, 4) he (the boy) will be in the same window with Richard, arms just touching, 5) he (the boy) will get the last line of this story, 6) the last line is *What a night sky*.

The boy is so confident that he will finally star in his own story (he realizes he has been left out before, amongst other things, that the two fathers are actually the same, poorly-realized character, both his father, too) that, at first, he pretends not to hear the sound of laughter rising from downstairs. Instead, he arranges a table where the three of them will sit and eventually discuss his parentage, resulting in the crisis moment, the unmasking (Burroway 7, Gardner 188, Macauley/Lanning 205). It will be difficult for all of them, but necessary for the resolution. Robert will cry.

So it confuses the boy when he now hears, amidst the laughter, the unmistakable tick-*clop*, tick-*clop* of a Ping-Pong ball.

The Ping-Pong Table

A surprise, even for Richard. He thought it was the dining-room table, until Robert unhooked the cover from the net, and gave him a puzzled look. It is just the kind of surprise the boy upstairs would have orchestrated had he not been so busy with everything else. Alas—something overlooked.

Richard explains the game to Robert, who, it turns out, is an astonishing learner. He returns tricky serves with a careful slice of the paddle and places his own shots with an expert touch. His rate of improvement is dizzying and impossible. But there he is, running Richard ragged. The arc of the ball over and across the net pleases Robert. Why? He looks to Richard for an answer, but Richard is too busy chasing shots, grinning in a way that makes both of them laugh. They laugh and laugh.

The Windows

Still open. But for what purpose? The boy goes to the largest window and closes it. Through the glass, the sky looks unspectacular, gray. The interior lights make it look like the boy is sitting inside and outside the window. Normally this kind of observation—mirroring, doubling of the interior and exterior worlds—would thrill him, but now it does little for him. In its place, a darker thought: I will never have a name.

A Blend of Styles

Richard: short, choppy shots that squeak over the top of the net.

Robert: slow, looping lobs that create a gorgeous arc across the net.

Richard: an economy of movement, arm stiff and close to his side, feet planted apart, waiting.

Robert: chases one shot to the far right of the table, then runs to the opposite side, huffing, loose.

Richard: suspicious of Robert's style, certain he will win.

Robert: uncertain about Richard's approach, but already incorporating his defensive stance.

Richard: accidentally hits an arcing lob, and is amazed.

The score: tied.

Alex

The boy's name, never used. Here is everything Alex loves—it is too late for everything Alex loves. Alex puts his head to the table. It feels cool, welcoming. He would like to feel sorry for himself. He would like that very much. So he tries. What was it that he loved so much about this house anyway? The windows? The lights?

Downstairs, the Ping-Pong noise ceases. Silence. Alex understands.

Someone has won the game.

HE COULD PLAY THE CLARINET

Maybe he was never really all that nice to me; sure, I can admit that. Maybe he was always a little rude. Maybe he was mean. Maybe he said things he shouldn't have said, like the time he told me not to hold my chin a certain way, since the way I sometimes held it made it look like I had double chins—I can see that now as something he shouldn't have said, yes, I can. And maybe he stole fourteen thousand dollars from me over the course of a year. Maybe he snored during sex sometimes. Maybe his middle name wasn't Xavier, the way he once told my mother it was, and maybe he pretended to have a coughing fit when I tried to ask him about it later.

Maybe he was drunk for most of our relationship. Maybe his showers were infrequent. Maybe he had no friends whatsoever, and maybe his third ex-wife once spray-painted ASSHOLE across his garage door, and maybe the cops came looking for him that one time, and maybe he asked me to hide that shotgun in the crawlspace behind the sectional, but I'll say one thing for him: he could play the clarinet. He could play the clarinet like no one else. He really could.

Maybe he made some mistakes; I think in some way he understood that, no matter what anyone else says. Maybe he bought too many scratch-off lottery tickets. Maybe he shouldn't have stolen that Christmas tree, even if it was Christmas day, and someone had left it in the parking lot, a yellow "sold" tag turning in the wind. Maybe I should have said something when I found those emails from his coworker, the ones about him being her tiger and her being his little naughty cub. Maybe his toenails were long and sharp. Maybe he never flossed. And maybe he lied about what happened to my new Prius; I never did hear of black ice in August, but maybe he did try to steer the car clear of the ditch, the one that tipped the car on its side and forced him to escape through the passenger window before the cops showed up.

Maybe he once sort of hit on my mother, and maybe he never remembered my birthday, and maybe he wasn't as mindful of his flatulence as he could have been, and maybe his breath always smelled like hot dogs, but I know one thing no one could ever say: that couldn't play the clarinet. Because he could play the clarinet. He could! He'd close his eyes and move his fingers across the keys and make that clarinet sing.

And maybe there are things about him I'll never tell anyone, like the time he chained me to a radiator, or the time he ditched me in Atlantic City, or the time he laughed when I fell down the fire escape, or that one time he got his coworker pregnant—sure, those are all things I'll keep to myself. And maybe you could say, all in all, that he was the worst person that ever entered my life, and maybe you could say that I would have been better off having never met him at all, and maybe you could say that my subsequent therapy sessions and hospitalizations are mostly his fault, and maybe you'd be onto something; I think I could say that now, how you'd be a little bit right saying those things. I can see that, I can.

But here's one thing I know, and it's something I will always know, no matter what anyone else says and no matter what anyone else thinks about him: he could play the clarinet. He could play the clarinet like playing the clarinet was the only thing that mattered in the world. If you heard him, you'd know.

DON'T BE THAT WAY

Don't be that way. Be the opposite. Be strong. Be the person I always knew you to be, the one who loves autumn light and Arby's. Don't be the kind of person who says, "Let's fire up the grill!" I don't know why you'd want to be that kind of person.

Be a little bit your mother and a little bit your father, too. But not too much. Be the person you were meant to be. The person who keeps loose change in a broken dish and reads Sylvia Townsend Warner. The person who's a little in love with the past but is warming to the present, too. Don't be the kind of person who doesn't warm to the present. Get out, every once in a while. Walk in crowds and feel yourself deeply loved. That's a good way to be sometimes. But don't overdo it. Don't be sentimental. Don't be the kind of person who collects commemorative dinner plates. Or figurines.

Be the one who re-shelves mislaid library books, just because. The one who frequents city parks. Don't be the kind of person who doesn't frequent city parks. If something is funny, be the first to know it. Don't be the kind of person who never catches on when something is funny.

Do unflattering impressions of everyone you love, but do them in secret. Get them right. Get the way your brother always begins his sentences with, "In point of fact," whenever he's been challenged. Do that crazy wringing thing he does with his hands, too. You should know what I'm talking about. Don't be the kind of person who doesn't notice things. Don't be that way.

Take yourself seriously, but only up to a certain point. Wear your socks a size too small. If a driver signals you to cross the street, don't cross; another car could be coming in the other lane. Don't forget about the other lane.

Ask about the specials. There might be something you'd like on the specials and you'd have no idea if you didn't ask. Be assertive in an apologetic, self-deprecating sort of way. Make jokes with checkout baggers. Pray without ever mentioning it. Don't think that shoving all the dirty silverware into a glass and filling the glass with soapy water is the equivalent to washing the silverware. It isn't. Be the kind of person who washes the silverware right away.

Understand that the person you will become is already shaping itself around you. Be the kind of person who doesn't fear the future. But don't be foolish about it either. Strike a balance. Don't be the kind of person who never really strikes a balance. Be the other kind or person.

Be yourself.

MONKEYSHINES

It's hard to say when we realized our son had monkeyshines. My wife always claims she was the first to notice, and I guess that's true, since she was the one who called me over to his bedroom door one afternoon when he was supposed to be taking a nap. "Look," she whispered, and opened the door slightly. There was our son, clearly awake, clearly not napping, his baby hands reaching defiantly for the mobile that orbited above his pillow. His face wore a toothless smile.

"My god," I whispered.

My wife brought a hand to her mouth. "You don't think it's—"

"I don't think it's anything," I said. But I knew. In a way, I think both of us knew: monkeyshines. But we didn't want to say it.

And then, a few months later, there was the incident at the high chair. My wife was feeding our son from a jar of Gerber's, when our son pointed to the picture of the Gerber baby and said, "Abee!" My wife pretended not to hear, but it was no use; he said it again, "Abee!" My wife dropped the spoon and turned to me, but I didn't know what to say. She began to cry. "What are we supposed to do?" she said. Her shoulders trembled. "Oh, what are we supposed to *do?*"

Weeks passed. We both talked about it without really talking about it somehow. My wife borrowed books from the library, staying up late into the night, two pillows propped behind her worried head. I tried to reassure her, even when our son chewed on his stuffed animals, or balanced himself against our coffee table, or cried for what seemed no justifiable reason. My wife visited websites, blogs, and chat rooms. She bought our son a special set of building blocks, but he only stacked them into towers, then knocked them to the ground and laughed. His laughter was chillingly out of proportion to the event.

"I've about had it with these monkeyshines," my wife said.

"Honey," I said, "don't jump to conclusions."

"I'll jump to wherever I want to," she said.

I didn't know what to say to that.

One afternoon our son liberated himself from the coffee table and took three wobbly steps toward us. He raised both arms, as if for balance. "Abee!" he said. He was missing one sock, the other dangling loosely from his pale toes. His smile was limned with drool.

"Oh!" my wife said.

"Easy now," I said.

In the moment before he fell, our son gave us a look I can only describe as monkeyshineful. But I scooped him off the ground nonetheless and handed him to my wife, who was fighting back tears. "That's it," she said. "That's really it."

So we took our son to the doctor. The doctor placed him upon an examination table fitted out with crinkly white paper, peered into his ears with a flashlight, tapped his knees with a rubber tomahawk, and placed a stethoscope about his chest and back, all while our son screamed and cried and tore the crinkly white paper with his chubby fingers. Afterwards, the doctor scribbled something onto a clipboard, while my wife dressed our son back into his clothes.

"I'm afraid it's a rather bad case of—" our doctor began.

But my wife burst into tears.

"Monkeyshines?" I said.

The doctor nodded and capped his pen. "Monkeyshines," he confirmed.

My wife collapsed into my arms. I held her close. "We can get through this," I said. "Okay?"

After a moment, she wiped her eyes and whispered, "Okay."

And that's what it was: okay. It was okay when our son began walking about the house, twice nearly falling down the basement stairs; and it was

okay when he mastered climbing from his crib, for we knew the source
of these developments and we understood, as we understood when our
son started to repeat phrases from the books we read to him or smiled
when we made faces that weren't actually all that humorous, or when he
enjoined us to play round after round of peekaboo long after the game
had become tiresome and dull. Monkeyshines. We'd grown accustomed
to them, in a way, although we couldn't admit it.

"It's funny what you can get used to," I mused one night at the dinner
table as our son used a fork to bring solid food to his lips.

"Yeah," my wife said, and handed him a glass of milk. "Funny."

One day a few months later, my wife called me upstairs to the master
bathroom. Her eyes were wide, her face a mystery I wasn't able to solve.
"What is it?" I asked, but she raised a finger to her lips. She was standing
outside the bathroom door, which she opened just enough so that I could
see our son sitting on the potty, his pull-up diaper lumped around his
ankles. He was playfully kicking his legs and singing a song about fruit
salad. A moment passed, albeit a significant one. Then he stood from
the potty, pulled his diaper back into place, turned on the faucet and
performed all the necessary ablutions. My wife began to cry. Some imp
tightened a wrench around my throat.

"What will we do?" my wife said.

I didn't know what to say. For as much as we had suffered and endured
our son's monkeyshines, nothing had prepared us for what was next: *shenanigans.*

THE FAN

With the money he'd gotten for his eleventh birthday, William bought a fan.

"Is that supposed to make me feel bad?" his father asked, as William hefted the fan into their shopping cart. William and his father were at Home Depot, pushing a cart full of paint cans, paint rollers, and brushes. Their air conditioner had broken at the beginning of summer, back when William's mother still lived with them. Back before William's father began repainting all the rooms in the house. William's room, once white, was now cornflower blue with lavender trim.

"It's just a fan," William said.

"Because it seems like you want to make me feel bad," his father said.

William turned the box so that its price tag faced out. "It's on sale," he said.

"I no longer understand what anyone expects from me," his father said.

On the drive home, they passed a chicken truck with tiny white feathers trailing behind it.

The fan had three speeds and an oscillating head, which made it sometimes turn air upon places where William and his father weren't, like the corner of the kitchen, where his mother used to lean her mop, or the space behind the TV, which his mother had never allowed them to watch during dinner, as they did now.

"I've about had it with that fan," his father said.

"Keeps things cool," William said, and the fan, as if to prove his point, turned upon them both, and blew William's napkin from his lap.

"I'm not a fan of that fan," his father said, but William didn't say anything.

At night, William put the fan at the foot of his bed. He liked the way it blew his curtains against the window and fluttered his posters from behind their tacks. He liked the sound it made. In the morning, William was always surprised to find he'd turned the fan off during the night. He could never remember doing so.

William's mother called him on Saturdays. William's father let him use the phone in the study he was never allowed to use otherwise. William sat at his father's desk and waited for the phone to ring, which it always did at exactly four o'clock, since this was the time his mother had arranged with William's father. At four o'clock on Saturdays she would call William and William would answer the phone he was never allowed to use otherwise and say, "Hello?" William always felt a little foolish saying hello since he knew who was calling. His mother must have known that it would always be William answering on the other end—who else would it be?—but always answered him by saying, "William? It's me, your mom." Then she would ask him what was new and he would say nothing, even though he was holding his face just inches from the fan.

One morning William and his father painted the master bedroom. William's father allowed him to stir paint with a wooden stick and later had him hold one end of a king-sized mattress as they scooted it out into the hallway. "This mattress is heavy," William said.

"This mattress is where you got your start," his father laughed. William felt embarrassed.

By afternoon it was raining. Hard. William moved the fan away from the bedroom windows, positioning it towards the drying walls. "That's not going to do much," his father said. William shrugged. It felt strange to be in the bedroom with his father. He kept expecting his mother to walk in, but that was a stupid thing to expect. He set the fan to the highest speed and watched his father paint the ceiling with a long roller. The ceiling light flickered whenever lightning fell nearby. The storm worsened.

The electricity went out.

William looked at his father, but his father was watching the fan, which still turned along its course, defying logic, defying science, defying everything, until its blades whirred to a halt, and William knew she was gone.

WAS THAT THE TIME WE WALKED THROUGH A FIELD OR "THE MOST DANGEROUS GAME"?

It was hot out, that's for certain. We hadn't dressed properly for a long afternoon walk, especially on an unmarked path, as this one was, with tire tracks disappearing into the mud and cows lingering beneath low trees. *They can't hurt you*, you said, but I didn't say anything. I didn't want to go for a walk. You knew that. I was happy sitting by the lake where kids shouted from Jet-Skis. It was that kind of lake. Or it wasn't. Was it the ocean instead? Hadn't I just washed ashore, my boat lost at sea? My clothes seemed torn. I wandered through the forest, following the path that led to your mansion. Just the kind of place I'd expect from you: extravagant, excessive, lit by torches.

"You have some wonderful heads here," said Rainsford as he ate a particularly well-cooked filet mignon.

I wasn't afraid of the cows, really. But there were so many of them, so few of us. Do the math, I said. Orange tags hung from their ears. Remember that? My idea: run the length of the fence before they noticed us. Your idea: walk right through them, following the path. But weren't you hunting me then? Didn't the path disguise a trap whereby I'd impale myself on several lengths of sharpened sticks? A tiger trap. Wasn't that your plan? I followed you anyway.

The pent-up air burst hotly from Rainsford's lungs.

Up close, I could hear the cows breathing. Their fur matted with briars. They regarded us like we were the idea of something they already knew.

Wind, perhaps. You cupped your hands to you mouth. *Moo*, you said. Cows, formerly sitting, stood. Tails swished. I began to run. For my life, I would have said, had you thought to ask.

"Nerve, nerve, nerve!" he panted as he went along.

The fence was high, but I managed to jump it. Or was it an ocean cliff? Didn't I feel myself falling from an impossible height? Didn't I pierce the water like a flung coin, rising, then gasping for air? Didn't you think me gone?

"Rainsford!" screamed the general. "How in God's name did you get in here?"

That night, we stayed up late playing cards, drinking beer. You lost several hands to me, on purpose, I thought, by way of apology. It didn't matter. We cooked fish over an open fire, something that had always been on my list. Then S'mores, because those were also on the list. It was cool out, starry. The stars seemed to say, *You've won. You've won again.*

Or was that you, dealing another round?

He had never slept in a better bed, Rainsford decided.

ROOM HISTORY

The parents call it the family room, and carpet it with thick shag, popular then, although their children will later ridicule them for it. How could you pick *that*? they tease. The children do not remember the carpet, although a half dozen photos of them crawling across it reside within the family photo album. What the children remember is the way light slanted in from the room's sliding glass doors. In winter, the doors shouldered squat drifts of snow.

A television presides in the corner between the sliding glass doors and a narrow bookcase. When the parents replace the shag with Berber, the television remains, as does the bookcase, although several titles—*Bloodline, Chariots of the Gods?, I'm OK, You're OK*—are lost to garage sales and library donations, their places now occupied by *Pet Sematary, Iacocca*, and *The Clan of the Cave Bear*. Along with these changes comes another: the children are sometimes allowed to eat dinner in the family room while watching TV, which they enjoy, the two of them sitting on a gray blanket the mother sets out for them, although these meals complicate their notion of the room: is the family room still the family room when it doubles as the dining room? The family room, by virtue of sheltering the TV, threatens to eclipse the kitchen, the sun around which all the house's other rooms have always seemed to orbit—but no more. The children finish their meat loaf in the radiance of *Happy Days* and *M*A*S*H*.

By the time the children enter high school, the room has accommodated fourteen Christmas trees, the most recent a blue spruce that the father insists has left needles inside the clothes dryer. The old Wyeth print above the fireplace has yielded to a watercolor one of the children painted in sixth grade, a long swing descending from a splotchy oak. The room is also the occasional refuge for Shazam, the family Siamese, a replacement pet for Max, a tabby, although no one could have foreseen Shazam's longevity, going on twelve or thirteen or fourteen this year, over a decade now of Shazam hiding beneath the family room sofa for what seems days on end. The sofa is from IKEA, as are the coffee table and new bookshelves, dark black and reflective as mirrors when the sun strikes them from the sliding glass doors. A prom photograph is taken in the room, as are a few graduation photos, the tree swing watercolor just visible behind the graduate's mortarboard. Family room photographs tend to run to dark and swap out pupils for bright red dots. When no one is looking, the room acquires plantation shutters.

After the children depart for college, the mother moves her old sewing table into the room, between the fireplace and the sliding glass doors. At first she sews frequently—two skirts, one shoulder bag, four blouses—but the noise bothers her husband, who has already transformed the daughter's bedroom into an office and fitted it out with a TV that blasts ESPN and CNN. He begins spending more time there, and after a while, does not think it strange to carry his dinner upstairs and eat it in the company of SportsCenter. The mother prefers the television in their bedroom, a good place to watch PBS miniseries without her husband's censure, and not nearly as drafty as the family room in the wintertime, which has never been properly insulated. The two televisions draw the mother and father into separate rooms, something the children whisper about, on holiday visits, their parents growing older and stranger to them, they agree, as is the family room, which their mother has inexplicably burdened with her old sewing table. The children sleep in their old rooms; the daughter must make do with the sofabed in her father's office. Will their parents separate?

Years later, when the first grandchildren arrive, the parents—now grandparents—cordon the family room off with a baby gate, remove the coffee table, and clutter the room with toys they buy at garage sales and consignment shops: Leap Frog tables, Melissa and Doug easels, Thomas the Tank Engine train sets, a KidKraft Grand Gourmet Corner Kitchen, and a Hippity Hop ball the grandchildren keep caroming off the sliding glass doors. The grandparents say they don't mind; their children accuse them of being too lenient, too soft. *When did you ever let us play in here?* they say. *We were never allowed to do anything in this room!* One grandchild is frantically stirring an omelet comprised of wooden eggs, plastic ham, and Velcro bacon. Another grandchild slams a smiling train into another smiling train. The room holds shouts, screams, and laughter.

This room was dull, their children say. *Nothing ever happened here.*

WHEN I HEARD ABOUT
THE TROMBONE

I'm not the kind of guy who goes looking for trouble, but when I heard about the trombone, I knew I had to do something. People had been talking about it the night before at the bar. I could hear them as I chalked my pool cue and lined up my shot. It was all trombone this and trombone that, even though everyone pretended like they hadn't been talking about it. They drank their beers and laughed like they didn't know a thing about the trombone. But I knew. I knew what had happened and why and who was responsible. I could see their guilty little faces as plainly as I could hear a trombone playing in my head.

I left the bar and drove to Freddy's apartment. It was late, but I could hear the TV turned up loud the way Rita, Freddy's girlfriend, always liked it—so Rita was there. When I knocked, someone muted the TV. I heard whispered arguments, furniture being moved, and what sounded like a chair crashing to the floor. Freddy's face, behind the security chain, was pale, puffy, and mottled with stubble.

"Try shaving," I said, but before Freddy could say anything, Rita pushed him aside and pointed a finger at me. "Stay out of our lives!" she screamed. "We don't know anything about it! Stop bothering us!" She was wearing an ugly pink bathrobe that seemed recently stained with slide oil. Through the aperture of the chained door, I could see a trombone case hastily stuffed beneath the coffee table.

"That empty?" I said, and gestured toward it.

Rita slammed the door in my face. "Get out!"

"Yeah," I heard Freddy say, "and don't go bothering Aloysius, either!" and then I heard Rita punch Freddy and Freddy say, "Ow, why'd you do that?"

Aloysius. Of course.

When I found Aloysius's house, his mother was in the kitchen fixing him his warm milk, the way she sometimes did after a long night of practice. Steam rose from a heated saucepan. Aloysius's mother invited me to sit at the table, where stacks of what looked like sheet music had been hurriedly flipped facedown. "Junk mail?" I said.

His mother handed me a trembling mug of milk and said, "Oh, just this and that."

"Familiar tune," I said.

Upstairs, I found Aloysius in his bedroom, feigning sleep, although he'd neglected to turn off his desk lamp, bright enough for me to see the mouthpiece he'd pathetically tried to hide beneath his bed. I palmed the mouthpiece and punched him in the arm. "Ouch!" he said. His breath was lousy with warm milk. "Listen, I don't know what Freddy told you, but—"

"Save it," I said. Aloysius was wearing his headgear, his forehead freckled with acne cream. His eyes were dark seeds. "Tell me," I said.

"Did my mom give you milk?" Aloysius said, but I grabbed him by the headgear and began to twist. "All right! All right!" he hissed. "Jeez! It was Tito, okay? Are you happy? Tito did it. God!" He made little whimpering noises. "You don't have to be such a bully all the time."

I stood from the bed. "Most days," I said, "I think I'm the nicest guy I know."

It was the early morning when I got to Tito's place, but the door was unlocked like always. Tito was sitting in his La-Z-Boy, his pet ferret, Franz Xaver Sussmayr, wrapped around his shoulders like a poorly knotted scarf. "Sit, Sussie!" Tito said when the ferret lunged for me. "Can't you see our hero has arrived?" The ferret nipped at my shoes and made a noise like sausage frying. "You'll have to forgive Sussie," Tito said. "We are not used to visitors, are we, Sussie?" Tito pulled Sussie back with the thin rope tied around his neck—his whole body was a neck, really—and hooked the rope to a zip-line strung across the ceiling. The ferret darted down the hallway, the line whirring in his wake.

"Now, where were we?" Tito asked.

"About the trombone," I said.

"Ah," Tito said. "Yes, about the trombone." He reached beside the La-Z-Boy and raised the trombone to his lap. Its tubing had been newly polished; the bell glistened and shone. "Do you know what I asked Sussie this morning?" Tito said. He worked the slide, warming up. "I asked him what he had done for his country lately." Tito laughed his tuneless laugh. "Now, isn't that a funny thing to ask? But a good question, nonetheless, I think. Even though I've since wondered how I would answer. That's what I was thinking about when you came in. How I would answer." Tito looked at me. "How would you answer?"

I reached in my pocket, grabbed the mouthpiece, and tossed it to Tito all in one motion. He caught it with his repulsively large hand. "Perhaps one last song?" Tito asked. "For Sussie?"

I considered this. "OK," I said. "One last song."

Tito inserted the mouthpiece, raised the trombone to his lips and played. Sussie ran the length of the house, through the rooms and up and down the hallways, in what was surely a dance.

WHAT DID WE DO TO THE HARDINGS?

The Hardings were our neighbors for a little over three months, although we didn't know them very well. No more than any other neighbors, really. The truth is that we had very little to do with Hardings, aside from the familiar things you might expect between neighbors in a suburban community like ours, whose streets all bear the names of composers and whose lone playground is one of the few places we can recall seeing the Hardings on anything like a regular basis. The Hardings had their lives; we had ours. Still, we find ourselves thinking about the Hardings more than we'd like to admit.

There were four of them: Jim and Marjorie, the parents, and their two children, Brenna and Colt. On the day they moved in, we baked them a pumpkin loaf and left it on their doorstep. We'd left a little note from the children, too, whose cheerful misspellings and poorly drawn people aimed accidental frowns at the Hardings. The bread was still warm when the Hardings knocked on our door and said thank you, what a nice surprise. We said it was nothing at all: would they like to come over later for a drink?

They would, they said. They would like that very much.

How about seven? we said.

Seven would be great, they said.

Around six-twenty they showed up, sweating and of breath. We had to move the piano, they explained.

Oh, we said. The piano!

"Fucking movers," Jim said. "Can't tell a fucking family room from a fucking living room."

"Jim," Marjorie said. "Please."

"They get paid just the same," Jim said. "Isn't that the truth?"

We agreed that movers could be a real pain. We told them a not entirely true anecdote about the movers who broke our antique buffet (it only needed a leg retightening) and asked Colt and Brenna if they wanted to go upstairs and play with the children.

"Oh, they want to," Jim said. "They'd run away from home if we didn't lock them in each night."

We laughed, but Jim and Marjorie didn't. Instead, they gave us a look I'll never forget, a look that somehow conveyed equal parts contempt, fear, and abhorrence. Then Jim said, "Well, thank you for this lovely evening," and Marjorie called upstairs for the children. "Kids, we're leaving!" she said, and the next moment Colt and Brenna stomped down the stairs and marched through our front door without saying a word. My wife asked if they would like to stay a bit longer, but Jim held up his hand and said, "Thank you for this lovely evening," and then shut the door behind him.

For days and weeks afterward, my wife and I talked about what had happened. What had we done to drive the Hardings away? Why were they so angry? Why did they react to our laughter that way, when they were the ones who made the joke, not us? It didn't make any sense whatsoever. None. Still, we couldn't help feeling that we'd done something wrong, some offense we were certainly guilty of, even if we didn't know what it was or what it meant. We replayed the conversation over and over again. We recalled them closing the door and storming away. What did we do to the Hardings?

We saw them a few times before they moved away. They were always pleasant enough, but not exactly friendly, either. If we made small talk, they would answer our questions (yes, it has been cold lately; no, they weren't planning on traveling this summer, etc.) but never asked us anything about our lives. Colt and Brenna would not venture into our yard, even to retrieve a soccer ball or Frisbee. Jim and Marjorie never waved. For a long time after the Hardings moved, I imagined that every phone call was them calling to explain what we'd done, but it never was, so eventually I stopped imagining that.

THE BOTTOM OF THIS

That afternoon my son's principal called me at work and said he'd like me to get to the bottom of this. I said what did he mean? He said, "I think you know what I mean." I told him I'd be there in half an hour.

"Make it fifteen minutes," he said.

When I arrived at my son's school, I could see that most of the children were already standing in the parking lot. Teachers barked instructions through megaphones. A crossing guard marshaled preschoolers across the sidewalk. When I tried to enter the visitor's lot, a police officer motioned for me to turn around.

I rolled my window down and said, "He's my son, officer."

The officer peered into my car and gave me what seemed a pitying look, his eyes masked behind mirrored sunglasses. "Then I hope you can get to the bottom of this," he said.

When I entered the main office, the administrative assistant hurriedly got off the phone and offered me a false smile. "How can I help you today?" she chirped. But her voice was shaky.

"I'm here," I said.

She handed me a pass and said, solemnly, "The principal wants you to meet him outside the multi-purpose room."

Outside the multi-purpose room, the principal was stringing a chain lock through the doors. "To be on the safe side," he said, and then handed me a length of chain. Behind the doors, I could already hear Jeremy crashing into things. A stack of lunch trays or books or sporting equipment fell like a thunderclap. He was whistling, the way he sometimes does when he's nervous.

"Let me talk to him first," I said.

"That's the idea," the principal said, and chained the door behind us.

It only took me a second to see what the problem was: they'd installed skylights in the multi-purpose room ceiling. "We've got to get him away from those," I whispered, but at that moment Jeremy flew by. His sneakers had already fallen off, his socks revealing holes I hadn't noticed before. He soared toward the skylights. "Open the fire exit doors!" he shouted, the moment before he smacked into a skylight. "Please!"

We opened the fire exit doors. But Jeremy only battered against the skylights again. A moment later he swooped across the lunch tables and perched atop a basketball backboard. "I think we've all done our best, Dad," he said. "You, me, Mom, Principal Stephens, everyone." His breath heaved in his chest. His hair was slick with sweat. "But sometimes things get so overwhelming it's like I don't know what to do anymore. Do you know what I mean?"

I thought about the security bars across Jeremy's bedroom windows. The handcuffs and leg irons we hid whenever guests stopped by. "We'll get to the bottom of this, son," I said, but Jeremy only flew through the multi-purpose room, through the fire exit doors, and into the afternoon sky, and we never did.

AND PLUS

They met at the restaurant, and plus it was raining. She didn't look the way he'd remembered, but not too different, he supposed, and plus she was his estranged daughter.

"This rain," she said, but her father didn't say anything. Instead he moved uncomfortably to the back of the booth and squinted at the menu. The restaurant was Mexican, and plus she had called him.

She watched her father holding his menu upside down. A mistake, she thought, to meet at this restaurant. Should have met someplace else, someplace she knew, and plus she'd run away from home at seventeen.

He didn't like these new menus, always so confusing, with too many choices, too many strange ingredients, too many unfamiliar words. He'd forgotten his reading glasses again, and plus his wife had recently died.

His daughter told him about her life. How she'd gotten things back on track after her last divorce. How she was putting things in order now. She had some regrets, she said, but who didn't? She offered a hopeful smile, and plus she needed to ask him for money.

Her father shook his head. "These crazy words," he said. But he kept reading the upside-down menu. She was telling him about her new job until the waiter materialized and asked if they'd like to hear about the specials. The father heard about the specials, and plus she was probably going to ask him for money.

A few minutes later their food arrived, sizzling, steaming.

"Very hot," the waiter said.

"Careful," the daughter said.

But the father grabbed the plate anyway, and plus his wife had told him not to give the daughter money again. "She'll never change," she'd said. The plate burned the father's fingers, and plus tears.

THE GOOD PHONE

We called it *the good phone*, the downstairs telephone mounted to the kitchen wall, to differentiate it from the only other telephone in our house: the green Trimline in our parents' bedroom. If we were upstairs and the phone rang, we would race to the bedroom, dive across the bed and try to answer by the third ring—this, a game of our own devising, a game we sometimes expanded upon, assigning meaning to the third ring, as in, *If we don't answer the phone by the third ring, the world will explode.* The Trimline had illuminated push buttons that glowed as greenly as fireflies. But the caller always sounded like they were trapped inside a tin can.

Usually the call would be for our parents. *Mom, Dad,* we'd announce. *Telephone!* We'd hear them rise from the living room sofa or family room sectional, and say, "I'll take it down here on the good phone." Then we'd listen until they'd picked up downstairs, their voices blooming in our ears. *Hello?*

The good phone had gray buttons and an ivory base. The receiver was heavier than the Trimline, perhaps one reason phone calls sounded so much better, clearer. The good phone had a long cord that twisted into complex loops and tangles; try to stretch them out and they'd only return in an instant. Later, in high school, when we had calls of our own—important calls, calls from boyfriends and girlfriends—we'd take those on the good phone. And, much later, after we'd moved out of the house, after we'd become adults, whenever we called home with disappointing news, news of parenting dilemmas, of marriages ending, of health problems and loss and sorrow and pain, our parents would always say, "Wait. Let me switch to the good phone."

ONCE YOU LEARN, YOU NEVER FORGET

At long last, after my son has graduated from college, married, divorced, and moved back home, I teach him how to ride a bike. We stand in our driveway, my son, Owen, frowning beneath his bulky helmet, as I explain how to balance, how to turn, and how to brake. I am explaining the gears when Owen cuts me off and says, "Jesus, Dad, I'm not a child."

"I know," I say. "I'm just trying to help."

"Do you want to know what would help?" Owen says, and rocks from one foot to the other, experimentally. "You not trying to help."

We are not close, Owen and I. We have had our differences. We have said things we wished we had not said, and done things we'd rather forget, our differences arising, predominantly, from me thinking and feeling one way about the world and Owen thinking and feeling the exact opposite. I tell him I am sorry; I will stop trying to help. Owen doesn't say anything, though. He just squeezes the brakes a few times and stares down the driveway, which slopes moderately enough to permit coasting without pedaling, but not steep enough to require hand-braking, something I would have pointed out in my pre-Promising Not to Help phase.

"Do you know what this reminds me of?" Owen says, and, before I can ask what, says, "Me chasing the basketball down the driveway whenever you missed a shot. Remember? You used to pay me a nickel for the ones that got stuck beneath parked cars." Owen snorts. "A *nickel*."

I tell him I do not remember that because I do not remember that. What I remember is Owen sending me bills for overdue allowance, the late fees set at exorbitant rates, seven dollars for making his bed, nine for brushing his teeth.

"It was hard," Owen says, "getting the ones that were jammed beneath the muffler." In the months leading up to his divorce, Owen and his wife, Vlada, would review my failings at the breakfast table and dinner, while watching TV or riding along with me to the supermarket, their car repossessed. "It's like the time you told Owen to gather kindling for the electric fireplace," Vlada would say, pointing to a neighbor clearing his yard or, upon me passing Vlada the salt, "Remember the time you told Owen the slugs would enjoy it?"

Now, I place one hand on the back of Owen's seat, the other on the handlebars.

"I weigh one hundred and seventy-eight pounds, Dad," Owen sighs. He pushes my hand away, and, in a sudden motion, brings his feet to both pedals, stands, and begins pumping. The bike rocks dangerously, a circus act upon a wire. Owen's expression is a mix of terror and resentment, the same one he turned on me whenever I tossed him into the deep end.

"Keep pedaling!" I shout. And it is only then that I realize I'm running alongside Owen's bike, my hand still holding the back of the seat.

"Let go!" Owen says. But I do not let go. I instruct Owen to keep pedaling. I tighten my grip and quicken my pace. I feel my heart beating in my ears.

"This is just like the time you followed me to my junior prom!" Owen cries, and I would remind him that he was the one who'd hotwired my Lexus if I wasn't breathing so hard and if I could remember the lie I told the cops when they pulled him over. Owen pumps his legs; I feel the bike begin to pull away. "Let go!" he says. "I'm not a baby."

I think about Owen in his baby crib, staring glumly through the bars, the blocks I'd stacked to spell DADDY knocked to the floor. I think of Owen's first Christmas home from college, observing, of the tree I'd twice tied and re-tied to the roof of our station wagon, "You always get a dead-looking one." I think of the time we argued for an entire car ride about whether airport "departures" meant the place where one departs from or departs the *plane* from, and whether "arrivals" meant the place one arrives after the flight or the place one arrives to board the flight.

I let go of the bike. Owen pedals. Owen rides. His helmet shimmers in the sun. I stand in my driveway, a father watching his son ride a bike for the first time, and wish someone could take a picture of the two of us together, but Owen leaves the driveway, and we're apart again.

THEFT

It's hard to say when my husband began stealing from me. The first thefts were so small, so slight, and so difficult to detect, that it's possible he'd been stealing from me for years without me knowing about it. Longer, even. I admit it took me an embarrassing amount of time to notice, so much time, in fact, that I hardly know what to do about it now. I really don't. Some days I find myself on the brink of confrontation, ready to accuse him as he slices carrots into a delicious Thai soup, or rakes the leaves from the flowerbeds so that the soil underneath can take the sun, or greets me after a long day of work with a freshly laundered towel, gym bag, and membership card, ready to get in a quick workout before we head off to the symphony together. But something holds me back. I don't say anything. I taste the soup. I watch him rake. I tie my running shoes and place the symphony tickets inside my clutch.

The first thefts probably occurred right after we met. I remember us talking after a morning of early-relationship sex, and he'd made a joke about knowing you'd crossed a certain relationship line when you felt comfortable enough to do it before brushing your teeth, and I remember laughing and agreeing with him, even though I could have sworn that was a comment I had made already. Sometime later, we'd sat watching movie previews together, and when the preview announced "this film is not yet rated," he'd leaned into me and said, "This film is not yet *a film*!" and laughed like he'd made up that joke, which I knew he hadn't, since I'd been saying that for years, along with saying, "And *that* was the greatest gift of all" after opening each Christmas present, something he also stole from me, and something I never mentioned either.

Once we got engaged, the thefts only worsened. We moved into an apartment together, where my husband stole my habit of leaving the shampoo bottles turned upside down so that the shampoo pooled near the spout, and where he adopted several of my routines without even acknowledging them, like dusting our bookshelves with an old undershirt while listening to Ella Fitzgerald, or stacking the magazines to one side of the coffee table so that we could rest our feet on the other side while watching reality shows together. If I asked him where he got the idea to mix sour cream into the mashed potatoes, he'd say he'd always mixed sour cream into the mashed potatoes. Same thing about wearing his scarf outside his coat lapel. Ditto for dark wash jeans.

After we got married, my husband's stealing continued, as much a part of our union as the baby slowly shaping itself inside me. We'd drive home from an evening of visiting friends, and my husband would express my opinions about the visit as if they were his own, like "I don't think I've made an actual friend since college," or "I never know what to say to Julia when Richard leaves the room," or "it really bothered me when Juan kept talking about cross training," or "I always feel like I have the exact same conversation with Tina," or "I hate when Julia does that thing where she teases you and then pretends like you're a horrible person for teasing back," or "why do we always end up talking about the farmer's market? What could we possibly have to say about the farmer's market? It's a parking lot full of *vegetables!*" Etc, etc.

When the baby was born, my husband showed me how to carry it using the method I'd already shown him, rocked it to sleep while singing the song I always sang, set the mobile to the speed setting I always set the mobile to, and nicknamed our baby Oogie, which had been my idea, ever since the time I held the baby to my chest after a long feeding and its stomach distinctly grumbled "oogie," something I'd told my husband about and something he claimed I'd never told him, even after he surprised the baby with a little baseball cap that had the nickname emblazoned across its front. My husband taught the baby to smile whenever he moonwalked into another room, a routine I used to do in high school, a routine I was sort of famous for—I remember my husband crying with laughter when I'd first told him about it.

The other day I was giving the baby a bath when I noticed something strange. Through a trick of the bathroom light, perhaps, the baby's facial features, which always looked more like mine—everyone said so, even my husband—now seemed more like my husband's. The slight protrusion of the bottom lip. The dazed-yet-watchful aspect of the eyes. The thin plume of towel-dried hair. I worked the towel behind the baby's ears. The baby laughed and turned my husband's smile to me, unaware of any crime.

OUR FIRST COUPLE

They appeared freshman year of college, Thomas and Lisa, our first married couple, materializing, it seemed, at one of those house parties where people crowded into a kitchen whose floor was slicked with beer, the countertop a checkerboard of red cups and black cans, the line to the upstairs bathroom snaking down the hallway, the toilet noiselessly refusing to flush. We marveled at our first couple, eighteen and married— eighteen! What had possessed them to get married at such a young age, we wished to ask, but didn't. How could we, when Thomas and Lisa were so funny, so attractive, and so much fun? That was the thing about our first couple: we really liked them. We did. Thomas was movie-star handsome, but without the least trace of vanity; Lisa was the most beautiful woman we'd ever met, we privately agreed, but she waved a dismissive hand whenever we tried to compliment her. "Oh, *please*," she'd say, and then release a beery belch. Thomas wore terrible jeans. Lisa's glasses were ten years out of style. Standing together in the keg line, Lisa would raise Thomas's shirt enough to reveal his embarrassing tattoo, and we'd laugh with them and agree that yes, it was an embarrassing tattoo, and then it would be our turn at the keg, where Thomas and Lisa poured us a perfectly-foamed beer.

We followed our first couple around the party, without trying to appear to do so. We liked doing that. We liked spying Lisa leaning into Thomas and whispering something in his ear, her hand cupped against the noise.

We liked raising a drink to our lips and glimpsing our first couple from the corner of our eye, talking to friends, friends like us, we knew, who were also following our first couple. Did our first couple know? Unlikely, we thought, since our first couple would never think themselves the center of attention. Thomas told self-deprecating stories while Lisa chimed in, saying, "It's true, all true. It's a miracle he can even dress himself in the morning!" Lisa would laugh, but with one consoling hand on Thomas's shoulder, which shook from Thomas's laughter.

Later, when the party crept into the morning hours, we'd gather on the back porch and smoke and watch the moon. We liked smoking on the back porch with our first couple, who enjoyed exhaling a plume of gray-green smoke that curled and twisted in the moonlight as much as we did. We talked and smoked, our first couple's exhalations mixing with our own, indistinguishable, ascending.

And, much later, when the last few people congregated around the living room, someone would ask our first couple to show us their wedding rings, and then Thomas and Lisa would shyly raise their hands, and we would say, "How beautiful!" but we knew the party was over.

BAD CAR

It didn't seem like a bad car, the father would have everyone know. Not with those low miles, new tires, and an interior still redolent of the assembly line, something the seller had pointed out when the father had first taken the car for a test drive. The car had driven wonderfully. Smooth. The sound system defied the wind rushing through half-open windows. The engine hummed and purred. Had the seller mentioned the car's exceptional handling?

On the first drive home, though, the father noticed that the faces of other drivers turned to him, often with angry looks, often with threatening or lewd hand gestures. Small children, seated in the way-back of station wagons, stuck out pink tongues. Teens, slouched behind the wheel of SUVs, waved middle fingers and shouted expletives. A small, elderly woman in a copper-colored Town Car tailed the father for half a mile, flashing her high beams and punching the horn in what seemed a loose approximation of "Take the A-Train." An entire van of special needs students pressed threatening notes to their windows, many with hastily drawn pictures of the car falling from cartoonish heights.

The father's family told him to take the car back. Why did the father buy such a bad car? What was he thinking? That's what the father's family wanted to know: what was he *thinking* when he bought such a bad car? "But it's not a bad car," the father began to say, before his wife tossed a small ceramic bowl at his head, before his daughter upended a coffee table, and before his son screamed, "Why can't you do anything right!" and then stormed upstairs. The family dog sprinted outside and peed on the car's rear bumper.

"Listen," the father said.

But his wife only threw him a pillow and blanket, and said, "You. Couch. Tonight."

The next morning, the father woke to discover that someone had spray painted DIE CAR DIE! across the car's hood, and that someone else (or was it the same person?) had etched the car's roof with a fairly complex scrimshaw of the car rising from the depths of hell, although the father had to ascend a stepladder to appreciate the devilish flames curling from the car's headlights. Two-dozen robins, with the regularity and indifference of lawn sprinklers, freckled the car with blue-white shit.

The father didn't care. He climbed into the car and started the engine. "Just listen to that!" he cried. He rolled the windows down. "Would you listen to that?" He honked the horn and turned the radio on. "And you should see the way it handles!"

His family materialized behind the front windows just in time to see the angry mob descend, their crowbars, golf clubs, rakes, two-by-fours, baseball bats, lead pipes and rifles ready to rid the world of the bad car for good.

NO ONE SAW

Kitchen, fifth-grade, early morning:
I was late for school, I guess, and was trying to eat a bowl of Frosted Mini-Wheats while shoving my Civics notebook into my backpack when I felt the bowl slip from my hands—whoosh, gone!—and the next thing I knew I'd managed to drop to my knees and somehow catch the bowl with the notebook, which simultaneously sent the milk and cereal into a sudden plume that shot into the air and then fell back into the bowl without spilling a drop.

High school hallway, freshman year, mid-afternoon:
The water fountain outside Mr. Olsen's biology lab always had the coldest water, and I remember I thought it would be a good idea to use that water fountain instead of the one outside Mrs. Scheer's classroom, where I'd asked to be excused to use the bathroom, even though I knew I wasn't really headed to the bathroom; I was headed to the water fountain outside Mr. Olsen's biology lab, which required me to walk all the way down the freshman hallway, past the trophy case, past the library, and then up the stairs to the sophomore wing where Mr. Olsen's class was still in session (I could hear him them watching a filmstrip, could see the blue-green light ghosting the small square window on Mr. Olsen's door) and where I re-member thinking how nice it would be to lower my head to the cold water and drink and listen to the filmstrip—and that's when the water fountain

knob came off in my hand, and the fountain began spewing cold water onto the sophomore hallway, which made tiny echoing sounds as I ran down it, double-timed the stairs to Mrs. Scheer's classroom, and returned to my desk with my heart beating in my ears.

Halloween party, college, early morning hours:
I didn't want to go to a costume party, especially one hosted by my ex-girl-friend, who had broken things off with me just two weeks before Halloween, and didn't plan on wearing a werewolf mask—a loaner from my roommate, who was off to a better, costume-less party—or a long sleeved flannel shirt, or brown furry gloves (I'd found these in the dormitory laundry room), or farmer's overalls, all things I never wore the entire time we were dating, and which likely explained why I was able to approach the keg line without her recognizing me, even when she filled my cup to the brim and I'd grunted thanks.

Gas station, first year of marriage, evening:
I told my wife I needed to stop at the gas station and get gas on the way home, which was true, but I didn't realize you could get a car wash for only three dollars, so I decided to get the car wash, too, and that's when I rolled up to the car wash lane, entered my car wash code, and pushed the start button, just like the instructions said, but the car wash never turned on, even after I pushed the button like eleven times, and even after I drove though, and even after I decided not to turn around and ask for my money back.

Realtor's office, three months before parenthood, lunchtime:
The thing was, we really enjoyed working with our realtor so much, and had so many good times viewing home after home after home with her, that when we finally closed on the house and signed the last of the last of the paperwork, I didn't notice, between laughs and hand shakes and hugs and congratulations and one more set of forms to initial, etc., that I'd accidentally pocketed our realtor's Mont Blanc pen, the one she'd told us her father had given her, and which I used for two days only—ok, three—before driving back to the realtor's office and sneaking it back to her desk when I knew she'd be at lunch and when I knew her administra-

tive assistant would be playing computer solitaire while spooning yogurt from a pink cup.

Changing table, first twelve months, 4:07am:
I admit that placing an alarm clock by the baby's changing table wasn't the best substitute for a proper nightlight, but I found a strange comfort in the clock's bright numerals, and sensed that the baby did, too, since he sometimes reached for the clock in the middle of a changing, and since he once said "four oh seven" as clearly as I would, even though I never told anyone and knew they wouldn't believe me if I did.

Two-lane highway, son's ninth birthday, evening:
We drove with the windows down and listened to classic rock radio, since my son liked to drive with the windows down while listening to classic rock radio, and since this was his birthday and since we were headed home from his birthday pizza party, and I turned the music up and realized, despite tapping my fingers on the steering wheel, and despite occasionally singing along with the lyrics, and despite everything I'd ever felt about classic rock, that I no longer enjoyed it, and never wanted to listen to it again, even as nostalgia—surprising news to me, although no one saw it coming, myself included.

DISPATCHES FROM A HOUSESITTER

The professor's dog wears an electronic collar. Each morning, as the handwritten notes left atop the kitchen countertop remind me, I am to fasten this collar around the dog's neck and let him roam the yard. Afterwards, I am to remove the collar and replace it with the dog's blue "walking" collar. Note, in parentheses: *sometimes we have to carry Piper across the driveway—he's afraid he'll get zapped!* At night, Piper, an aging Sheltie, follows me around the professor's house, releasing ponderous farts.

The professor's office: a spare bedroom fitted out with Ikea bookshelves, a roll-top desk, and a banker's lamp whose lone bulb goes out the moment I pull the cord. I open the desk drawer long enough to glimpse the boring nothing within: a few cheap pens, Post-It notes, paper clips, and a coin holder his daughter clearly made for him, some kindergarten art project involving a kiln and significant teacher oversight. Inside the coin holder: a book of stamps, a marble, eleven pennies, and a Halls cough drop, cherry flavored. The cough drop tastes like pennies. Surprising books: Dan Brown, *The Da Vinci Code*; Tina Fey, *Bossypants*.

The professor's wife owns thirteen pairs of pajamas, although every time I've met her she's wearing workout clothes. Yoga pants. Under Armour shirts. Merrell shoes. She is smart and funny and witty and always offers to make me a mojito, no matter the time of day, four things I like about her. Five: she never asks how my classes are going. The professor's wife rarely completes her sentences. She says, "Is that a new messenger bag or?" and, "Do you want to leave early, or?"

Sometimes the family Skypes with me, since the professor's daughter likes Skyping, something she does with her grandparents, too. She stares into the screen and calls my name and says, "You keep freezing!"

The plants were dead before I killed them more.

Sometimes I talk to Piper. I tell him I'm going to sleep on the couch again, since I can't accept the offer of the professor and professor's wife's bed. Piper yawns his aging yawn and injects the air with the smell of eggs. Nights, I stay up late, hoping for something salacious on HBO.

I don't know why the professor chose me. I am not a good student. I am barely pulling a B-minus in his class, and will probably have to withdraw mid-semester, due to financial reasons. I am not especially pretty. My conversation: a series of loose sentences fitted around pauses and ums. I don't even like dogs.

But each day I get a little more accustomed to the house, to Piper, to this neighborhood where people wave and water lawns and transport mulch in wheelbarrows. Each day I feel like I'm getting closer to something, even though I don't know what it is.

"Don't worry," I tell Piper, when I carry him across the driveway. "I've got you."

SOON HE WOULD HAVE AN OPINION OF IT

H e could feel it coming, his opinion of it. There it was, only a few
pages away, or a song or two later, or just another moment until the
credits rolled up the screen or the actors took a bow or the club turned
the house lights on and sent everyone home, ears ringing and bleary-eyed.
He could feel it pleasantly assembling itself inside him. How he enjoyed
the birth of his opinion, its contours only partially known, now, in the
moments before someone asked him what he thought and he would tell
them, his opinion revealing itself to him as he spoke. *Aha*! his opinion
always seemed to say. That, or, *Surprise*!

But what if no one asked him his opinion? That happened sometimes,
he had to admit, more often than not, really. No matter. He could volun-
teer it anyway, uninvited. He could zip up his jacket and place his hands
in his pockets and, as he headed out into the wherever, could state his
opinion, his breath blooming in the cold night air. He could remove his
hands at certain key moments, punctuating his speech. He could turn
his hands up, as if to say, *What was that all about*? Or he could hold up a
finger to count off an idea, as in, *Tell me one thing that film did right. Just
one thing.* Or, even better, he could post his opinion later, taking his time,
choosing this adjective and not that, trading in the butter knife of human
speech for the surgeon's scalpel of the written word. His opinion, upload-
ed, posted, Tweeted, Instagrammed, Snapchatted, took on the burnish
of the factual, the true, the accurate. How correct his written opinions

seemed. If only the film or book or concert would end so that he might get to his opinion sooner.

Of course, there would be other people's opinions—there would be no avoiding those. Other people might disagree with him. Other people might offer their opinions first, while he was still shaping his own, and then he would have to decide whether or not to agree with them. Sometimes, when he was listening to other people's opinions, he could feel his own shifting, subtly, so that when his opinion finally arrived, it arrived refined, changed, not quite what he thought he had in mind. Someone else might say, *They shouldn't have played so many slow songs*, when he was about to say, *The slow songs redeemed the fast ones*, and then his opinion would arrive and he would find himself saying, *They shouldn't have played so many slow songs, even if the slow songs redeemed the fast ones.* He'd put his hands in his jacket, searching for warmth.

At last, the curtain closed. The encore ended. The house lights came on. The band gathered their instruments and took long pulls from bottled water.

Well, someone asked him. What did he think?

And that's when he realized had no opinion at all.

A GLASS OF COKE

When I was growing up, there was a girl in my neighborhood who used to drink a glass of Coke every night before she went to sleep. She was my friend's younger sister; he was the one who told me about the glass of Coke. He was a just a neighborhood friend—we went to different schools and didn't see each other all that much throughout the school year—but we spent more time together in the summer, when school was out, mostly bored, hanging out at his house, trying to think of what to do next. That was the part I remember most about hanging out with him: always trying to think of what to do *next*. One time we dug a hole in his front yard with his father's post-hole digger, and then shoved a garden hose deep into the hole and ran the hose on full blast for an hour. Another time we threw golf balls at sparrows.

But—the glass of Coke.

It had to be a glass of Coke, my friend explained, otherwise his sister wouldn't drink it. Not a bottle, not a can. With ice. Don't even mention Pepsi. She drank the glass of Coke in her bedroom, where her mother left it on the nightstand before kissing her goodnight. The nightstand held a half dozen unicorn figurines and a display case crammed with trolls. The trolls had wild hair.

I didn't see his sister much, but sometimes she would come outside to see what we were doing, or remind her brother of something he'd promised to do by the time their parents got home from work. She was freckled and skinny. She rarely wore shoes. Sometimes she would say hi to me, but more often she would talk to her brother like I wasn't even there. I remember watching TV with her one time, the three of us seated on the family room carpet, just watching some dumb cartoon none of us even liked, but I was able to observe her from the corner of my eye. I watched her for a while, wanting to ask her about the glass of Coke, but I didn't say anything. The cartoon ended. My friend and I went outside, found sticks, and scratched all the bad words we knew onto his driveway.

Wouldn't a glass of Coke keep her up all night? Why not try warm milk instead? Did she brush her teeth afterwards?

I never saw my friend's parents much. His mother worked as a school-teacher; his father worked for Chrysler. His father had an office in the basement fitted out with all these tiny model cars—all Chryslers—that must have taken weeks to assemble. The basement office gave off a faint whiff of fabric softener. My friend's mother collected owls. One time she complimented me on my table manners, but she addressed me by the wrong name, and my friend didn't correct her, so I just said thanks. They had a dog for a while, and then the dog wasn't around anymore. Skip, the dog's name was, or Skipper, or Skippy.

Their house was always messy, but no messier than most houses with two kids, and, for a while, a dog. I remember watching my friend's mother fold laundry while watching TV in the kitchen—they had a TV in the kitchen, a novelty back then—without thinking it strange that there were shirts and pants and towels draped across many of the chairs in the house, or that the fireplace held a stack of magazines so high that I imagined them going up to the rooftop. *National Geographics*, most-ly, with their yellow spines; those, and squat, rectangular *TV Guides*, stuffed atop the grate. A Santa Claus candle rested upon the downstairs bathroom's sink, even in summer, the candle's wick guttered to almost nothing.

I don't know what happened to that family. I don't where they are now. I don't know what life is like for them since the children have grown up and, presumably, moved out of the house and into adulthood. I don't really think of them much. They were just a family in my neighborhood whose son I used to hang out with sometimes. They lived down the street. There isn't much to say about them, really.

Except for this: whenever I do think about them, I think about the girl and the glass of Coke. I see the glass so clearly that it seems I am the one bringing it to her, not her mother, that I am the one placing the glass upon the nightstand, where the glass leaves a ring of moisture, glistening. The glass is cold. So much ice. The girl smiles and raises it to her lips. The drink crackles and fizzes. *Thank you*, the girl says. *I can't sleep without it.*

For me, the girl is still drinking the glass of Coke. Please don't tell me what happened to her. I don't want to know.

IT WAS LIKE THAT FOR A WHILE

They met in college, when she was about to graduate and he was thinking about dropping out. She lived in an apartment above a dentist's office, and sometimes, on his way to see her, he would see patients coming out of the office—kids with their parents, mostly, their fingers clutching toy prizes, toothbrushes—and he'd feel strange about sleeping with her, even after he moved in, even after she helped him study for finals and he managed to graduate with a decent GPA. That was the apartment with the dormer window that never closed, admitting snow into the kitchen in winter. The apartment where his hands could never seem to get warm, and he'd wash the dishes in water so hot it pinked his fingers, and she'd say, *How can you stand that?* but he wouldn't say anything and later she'd dry the dishes with the striped towel knotted around the refrigerator's handle, and it was like that for a while.

They married and moved to the city. The city! The sense of it rising to greet him, on those mornings when he'd take the bus to work, his monthly pass encased in a plastic fob that doubled as a keychain. She worked at a nonprofit, where her coworkers were artists, musicians, and actors masquerading as employees. On weekends, they'd all hang out together, their bright chatter filling their city apartment, wide as a trailer, the windows gradually fogging against the force of their banter, as someone refilled drinks and someone else stood to use the bathroom just off the master bedroom, where everyone had heaped their coats on a bed tombstoned with large pillows. It was like that for a while: everyone laughing and drinking, the conversation a ball to be kept expertly in play, as the windows, once reflecting them against the city lights, clouded over at last.

When their first child arrived, they'd already moved to the suburbs. The father mowed the yard on weekends and edged the grass along the sidewalk, as he had seen his neighbors do; imitating what one's neighbor's did a new impulse as strange, insistent, and suddenly familiar as the baby's cries. New music, the mother thought, whenever she rocked the baby in her arms. The house acquired one hundred and fourteen board books. PBS injected their living room with quarreling locomotives. Weekends, the father would look up from mowing to see his wife knocking on the kitchen window, waving the baby's arm *Hi, Daddy!* and he would stop the mower and wave and realize he was tired and later that night he'd fall asleep in front of ESPN and it was like that for a while.

A second child arrived. They moved to a bigger house. The children grew. One day the parents realized they could leave the children at home while they went shopping, and the children would be fine without them; the children would eventually go off into the world, and it's been like that ever since.

YEARBOOK

We drew things in the margins of our notebooks. Stones' lips and tongue, The Who, our names in ALL CAPS. We had difficulty closing the n of new words, like *totalitarian* and *narcolepsy*. Penmanship betrayed us. We were attentive to our breath, which turned sour more often, we noticed, requiring Trident, Tic Tacs, or a glorious shot of Binaca Blast which could, when empty, become a kind of blow torch, a match held to its mouth. Fire thrilled us. We would like a special page here just for fire.

We were in love with everything, even leaves, trees, and sunlight across the playground, but folded loose leaf into paper throwing stars. We ate Fig Newtons and neglected to finish *Animal Farm*. We prayed on the sly.

We took a class trip to Philadelphia, pretending we weren't interested to ride a bus that had tinted windows and was neatly striped blue and green on the outside, like a sleek trout. Veteran's Stadium, lit, on the ride home, like a fantastic, flipped chandelier—bored us. The art museum stairs, ascended in twos and threes, a chore. We mocked the Liberty Bell. We mocked Ben Franklin, Betsy Ross. *Fuck Betsy Ross!* we said, between mouthfuls of freeze-dried ice cream, sealed in triangular foil packets whose tops could be resealed and popped like bubble wrap. *You'd like to!* we laughed.

"Keep it down, gentlemen," our chaperone said. *Gentlemen.* We could make our farts say *Oh, yeah?*

Downtown McDonald's a revelation, men sleeping in booths, the cashier's fingernails so long they curled in on themselves, like seashells. Outside the Academy of Music, gas lamps, flickering, wanly, in the daylight. The pretzel vendor who returned our change with the advice, "Stay young: don't get married." A white tampon, afloat in a brown puddle, plump with rainwater.

Coming home, our bus broke down a mile from school. We stood on the shoulder as cars passed at high speeds. "We could just walk," someone said. "It's not that far."

"Yeah, let's walk."

"Can we?"

"We'll wait for them to pick us up, gentlemen," our chaperone said. "We can't walk along a busy highway."

But we could. If we had to.

This knowledge, like finding your photograph in the yearbook. Herringbone jacket, striped tie; you've forgotten to hide your braces, and look out from the page as happy as you truly are.

QUESTION MAN

I'm picking up Samantha at the McDonald's near my ex-wife's yoga studio, when Question Man arrives. He's got his hands in his pockets, shivering, although it is September and warm, the sky cloudless, the McDonald's crowd predominantly in shorts and T-shirts, except for Question Man and me. I'm wearing the only suit I own, the suit I was married in. Question Man is wearing a blue hoodie and blue sweatpants, a fifty-something Smurf with untied Reeboks and poor posture. When he sees me sitting at the booth on the opposite side from where I normally sit and wait for Samantha while trying to avoid him, Question Man walks over and says, "You waiting for Samantha?"

I tell him that's none of his business.

"Look," Question Man says, "you don't have to get defensive; I was just asking a question." He wipes his sleeve across his face the way he sometimes does when he's dressed himself all wrong for the weather. Not that I can cast stones, what with the suit jacket sticking to my back, and the only dress shirt I own jabbing me stiffly in the neck."I wish you wouldn't show up when I'm picking up Samantha," I say.

Question Man gives me a questioning look. His eyebrows, in need of a trim, furrow. "So," he says. "Is that what this is all about? Samantha?" His breath is redolent of NyQuil. He sits down across from me.

"Don't," I say.

"If this is about Samantha, that's something I could understand." He takes a French fry from my bag without asking. His chin, up close, is mottled with sharp, gray hairs. "I've always wondered if this is something about Samantha."

"It's not about Samantha," I say.

"But it could be," Question Man says. He's reaching for more fries. "You've got ketchup?"

"No," I say.

"McDonald's has really gotten fancy lately," Question Man says, stuffing seven fries into his mouth at once. "Have you noticed? Old Ronald has gone upscale, he has."

"Look," I say, but at that moment I see Julie and Samantha pulling up into the space next to my car. Julie has recently re-married a neurosurgeon named Jimmy Carter, and has taken to driving Jimmy Carter's Hummer to our drop-offs. The Hummer slows into the space next to my Civic with all the ease of the QE2 docking beside a paddleboat. Yes, it bothers me; and yes, I work as high school math teacher; and yes, I feel this gives me the right to feel deeply and profoundly sorry for myself; and yes, Julie is beautiful; and yes, I'm still in love with her; and yes, his name really is Jimmy Carter.

"Is this about Jimmy Carter?" Question Man says. "Is that what this is all about?" Somehow, he's gotten hold of my chocolate shake. "Because I could definitely see this all being about Jimmy Carter."

"Leave," I tell Question Man.

"Leave? Because of what I said? About Jimmy Carter?" Question Man asks, but we both know he's just stalling so he can sneak three more fries into his interrogating mouth.

"Now," I say, but Julie and Samantha have already spotted us: Samantha is in her recital dress and shoes, her hair done up in the way Julie sometimes does it up for Samantha's recitals, revealing the pink earbuds wedged into Samantha's ears like bubble gum. When they stand beside us, I introduce them to Question Man, again, who turns his charmless smile upon them both and wishes Samantha good luck, but Samantha doesn't say anything because she's got her music blaring. Question Man stands and waves a friendly goodbye to us before holding the door for a baseball team that enters McDonald's the moment Julie says, "You're wearing the suit."

"Yeah," I say.

"How can it still fit?"

"I had it altered," I say, which isn't entirely true. The truth is I had the jacket altered, but had to get new pants, which had already been asked, too many times, to hold my expanding, middle-aged girth, four sizes larger than the day the suit salesman belted my waist with a yellow tape measure and said, to what sounded to my prenuptial ears like a twin pronouncement on marriage and tailoring, "It's all about the right fit."

"Jesus, Tom," Julie says. "You need to stop wearing the suit."

"But I like the suit."

"Well, stop liking it."

"Okay, will do," I lie.

Samantha is air-keyboarding something complex and furious in the McDonald's air, which is already heavy with grease and the shouts of the baseball team who, having the entire restaurant to choose from, sit down next to us, a few of them eyeing me, this guy in a suit talking to a beautiful woman whose daughter is presently working through one of the trickier passages from Liszt's *Sonata in B Minor*. A fat kid whose cap seems homemade points out Samantha to his buddy, whose laughter is mercifully subsumed by the din that accompanies the arrival of the baseball team's drinks. I tell Julie and Samantha to have a seat. Julie complies; Samantha follows.

"Could you tell her to take those off?" I say, indicating the earbuds.

"She's *your* daughter, too," Julie reminds me, before Samantha removes the earbuds anyway, places them inside her iPod case, and says, "So, did you tell him yet?"

"Tell me what?" I say.

Julie gives Samantha a look, then says, "I was going to tell you yesterday, when I saw you at the bus stop, but it slipped my mind." Yesterday, at the bus stop: me waiting for Samantha as Question Man pedaled by on a ten-speed whose front basket held an ugly puppy. The puppy's gaze, in passing, asking a puppy question that loosely translated as, But what *is* this?

"She's dumping me on you," Samantha says, flatly.

"I'm not dumping you, Samantha; how dare you speak to me that way? Is that any way to speak to your mother?"

Samantha shrugs. "It's one way," she says. Samantha is fourteen years old.

Julie explains that she and Jimmy have decided to take a long weekend in Palm Desert, where Jimmy likes to golf and "recharge his battery" from time to time, a trip they hadn't planned on taking until a break in Jimmy's schedule materialized suddenly, in an instant, a surprise storm that was now dragging them toward flamingos, health spas, and octogenarians swinging nine irons. Julie had planned to tell me yesterday, she says, again. Would I mind taking Julie for the next few days? This, not really a question, and my answer, "Of course, no problem," is not really an answer, since we both know I'll agree to anything, me still dumb and in love with Julie and only longing to please. Which it is, pleasing, like right now, Julie and I conferring together, deciding things, acting like responsible parents, even though responsibility has never been our strength, really. We are mutually irresponsible, doubly incompetent, joined at the hip in our utter failure to be anything vaguely resembling good parents. Another sign of our clear and obvious and genuine compatibility—one soul-sucking divorce notwithstanding.

Samantha snorts. "Little doggie Daddy. Roll over, play dead."

"Watch it," Julie and I warn. We look at each other, the two of us with the same finger raised, pointing at Samantha who shrugs and says, "Get a room already."

We do not get a room. We say our goodbyes in the parking lot, where poor Julie has to struggle to swing her incredibly well-toned legs up into Jimmy Carter's Hummer. I tell Julie she should be careful, driving that thing. Julie gives me look meant to suggest her sympathy and contempt for me, her infatuated ex, her hopeful non-hubby.

After Julie pulls away, Samantha and I get into my Civic, which still is missing the temperature control knob I keep meaning to get around to, even though I've got a pair of needle nose pliers I use to adjust the AC and heat. I'm pretty good at it, working the temperature control knob with the needle nose pliers. But that's not something I'd brag about to Samantha, who usually gets on me about things like replacing the temperature control knob, or not running the cutting board through the dishwasher, or not trying to clean the entire bathroom with only Windex and paper towels, or clearing my gutters of the acorns that have been there since last fall, or paying taxes, or eating a salad every once in a while. Would it kill me to eat a salad every once in a while? McDonald's, at age forty-one? Really? That's what Samantha always wants to know: *really*?

"They've got salads now," I say, as we're pulling out the McDonald's parking lot, where, inside, the baseball team has launched the World War Three of food fights. Cups fly. Big Mac wrappers, concealing payloads of crushed ice, sail across tables, booths. Happy Meal boxes careen off tow-headed heads. "Pretty good salads," I add. "You can get them with grilled chicken. Plus that healthy salad dressing you like. Paul Newman."

Samantha inserts her earbuds again. "But you don't order the salad."

That's true, I don't order the salad, because why would anyone, given the choice between a Quarter Pounder with Cheese Extra Value Meal or a Two Cheeseburger Extra Value Meal choose a salad? When I point this out to Samantha, Samantha says, "Don't forget your seatbelt." She begins fingering the final movement of Beethoven's "Appassionata" across my dashboard. "You need to check the air pressure in the rear passenger's side tire, too. I'd say you're at least eight pounds low. Ten, maybe."

I never wanted to be a math teacher. I always wanted to be—and there's the rub; I have no idea what I always wanted to be. I am not good at my job. I am not a good math teacher. This, the source of much of my unhappiness, at least according to Julie, who, before she became a yoga instructor, was also a math teacher, and was also not very good at it, and was also unhappy. But who is happy? No one, as far as I can tell, although Question Man keeps asking me what do I mean by "happy"? What do I mean by "happy"? I mean *happy*, that's what! But that's never enough for Question Man. Whenever I say that, he gives me a look I can't quite read and pedals away on his bike, which, in addition to the puppy in the front basket, often has the oldest boom box I've ever seen duct-taped to the frame. The boom box is the approximate size of a microwave. I don't know how Question Man can balance, but he does, the boom box blasting big band music or country and western. Sometimes he sneaks a little oldies in there, too, which is more my speed than big band or country and western, but not really my thing, either.

———

We are late to Samantha's recital. We are always late to Samantha's recital.

"Sorry," I say as we pull into the school parking lot, where I have to take a spot near the back, near two green Dumpsters. A kid in a knit cap is standing atop one of the Dumpsters, which is crammed with flattened boxes, trash bags. As we slow into our parking space, I can see him jumping onto the trash, trying to compact it, I suppose.

"Are you really?" Samantha says. "Sorry?"

"Of course I am."

"Of course you are," Samantha says. "My poor sorry daddy, in his old wedding suit, with his wife gone golfing with Jimmy Carter."

"Don't talk to me like that," I say, but Samantha has already opened her door and climbed out of the car. I can see the kid in the knit cap watching us, until he goes back to stomping the trash. He's good at stomping the Dumpster trash. He's done this before, you can tell.

"Did you see that kid?" I say as I catch up with Samantha, who is already across the parking lot and has already returned her earbuds to her ears. This, a sign that I am not to speak to her until after the recital, but I know she saw him, because I caught her glancing at him when I was racing to catch up. She even waved, but he did not wave back. His face was blank, indifferent. The face Question Man sometimes turns on me when I ask him what he thinks he's doing showing up at my house at midnight, me camped out on the family room sofa again, unable to sleep upstairs, which has tripled in size since Julie moved out, and makes me feel like I've been left to spend the night inside a shopping mall.

"Hey, Samantha!"

But Samantha is already inside the building, on her way to the auditorium where I will sit with all the other parents I always sit with at Samantha's recitals, all of them kind and decent and yet flawed and human and real as anyone else, whose collective gaze intends to say, *Glad to see you made it,* yet all the while screaming *You poor sap; has Julie dumped Samantha on you again?* I smile the smile I always smile when assaulted by the collective gaze and take a seat next to a woman working a camcorder, who turns to include my arrival in the film, something we both know she'll edit out later.

A few moments later Samantha walks across the stage and takes her place at the piano. She still has her earbuds on, and it takes the audience a nervous moment or two to realize she's waiting until the music stops before she puts her fingers to the keys and plays. Liszt's *Transcendental Etudes*. One of the most difficult works for piano in the repertoire, a piece out of range for most Julliard students, let alone Samantha, a seventh-year at the Sunshine Academy of Music, where Mozart and "Hot Cross Buns" preside, where the music director, Miss Sally, wears flip-flops and animal prints, and where the auditorium forever gives off the smell of damp mittens and Play-Doh. The audience watches, transfixed. Samantha's hands dart and weave. Samantha's fingers perform complex trills. Low chords thunder and crash; high notes clang like struck bells. Samantha hop-scotches across Franz's furiously chalked court like it was nothing at all, a child's game. Samantha's face, always difficult to read, radiates both fierce concentration and profound indifference. These keys, these notes, these angry fortissimos—how they thrill and bore her! I feel myself beginning to sweat, and remove the only handkerchief I own from my suit pocket and wipe my brow, as I did with the same handkerchief on my wedding day, the moment after the minister pronounced Julie and me man and wife.

It isn't until Samantha reaches the last etude that I spot Question Man in the back row. He's still wearing his sweatpants, but he's replaced the hoodie with a floral shirt, the kind of thing you'd wear once, on vacation, and relegate to the back of your closet forever after. If there's anything I despise more than Question Man showing up at Samantha's recitals— that, and Question Man following me to work in his tricolor Yugo—I don't know what it is. I'm thinking of what I will say to Question Man after the recital, the anger in my voice rising the way it does when Question Man shows up at the recitals, when I hear it. The tune I do not want to hear. The tune that sends ice across my forearms and creeps into my dreams. The tune that sends everyone's heads turning to me, Question Man included, who meets my eyes with what he intends to be a sympathetic look before I turn away and watch Samantha, who holds one finger raised above the keyboard, pecking the keys.

Skidamarink a-dink-a-dink skidamarink a-do.

A song from Samantha's childhood. A lullaby. How many times did Julie and I sing it to Samantha as we took turns rocking her in the rocking chair I still can't bring myself to throw away, no matter how many times Samantha hauls it to the curb?

Skidamarink a-dink a-dink-skidamarink a-do.

I watch. I sweat. I dream. I long for escape. I regret everything I've already regretted all over again. I regret my failures as a husband. I regret my failures as a father. I regret wearing my wedding suit to Samantha's recital again. I regret things I don't even know what they are and never will, aside from carrying the weight of my regret, heavy as ten thousand bowling balls.

Skidamarink a-dink a-dink-skidamarink a-do: I LOVE YOU!

The tune ends. Nervous clapping and applause. Someone is on their feet, whistling and cheering, giving Samantha a standing ovation, but it isn't until Question Man puts a hand on my shoulder that I realize it's me.

There is a woman at work, Anne. Anne teaches Social Studies and coaches the girls' track team, neither of which she does well, she laughs. Anne is married to a man named Kendall Kensington. Kendall is tall and tan and handsome and the most popular orthodontist in town—half my students are among his brace-faced fans—but Anne is unhappy. What Anne and I do is get together and not have an affair. That's what we do, we joke; we have the best not-affair you can have, the two of us seated close—but not too close—in the teachers' lounge, eating another lunch neither one of us is hungry for, or touring the hallways on the pretence of heading to the lounge for another cup of coffee, where the two of us linger by the water fountain near the gymnasium until a student approaches and we part like there's nothing between us—which there isn't. Except for how there is. Sort of.

"Let me tell you how our affair would go," I say. Anne and I are sitting in the lounge, alone, when we both really should be making photocopies, but oh well.

"Tell me," Anne says.

"It would start off great," I say.

"But then," Anne says.

"But then we'd start apologizing about everything all the time."

Anne says, "And then we'd apologize about how we're always apologizing about everything all the time."

"Right," I say, "and that would become the whole affair: the two of us sitting across from each other apologizing about everything."

"In hotel rooms," Anne says.

"In distant towns."

"On park benches."

"In canoes."

"In darkened theaters."

"We'd apologize in all of them," I say. "We'd just keep apologizing."

Anne says, "We would. We'd be sorry for how lousy we were at having an affair."

"We'd make fun of ourselves," I say. "And then we'd apologize for how we're always making fun of ourselves."

"There'd be no end to it," Anne says.

"None," I agree.

We talk until we can't talk without someone noticing us talking, and then we go back to whatever it is we were doing before we started talking, whatever that was.

After the recital, I drive Samantha back to my place, where this week's newspapers make tiny thunking sounds beneath my tires as we pull into the driveway.

"Why do you still get the newspaper?" Samantha asks. These, the first words she's spoken to me since the recital, the drive home a celebration of silence and awkward tension compromised only by the note Question Man left flapping beneath my windshield wiper: IS THIS ABOUT SKIDAMARINK?

"I thought you might like having it around," I say.

Samantha sighs. "Please don't do things *for* me, okay?"

"But I like doing things for you," I say. "Remember all the fun we used to have reading the comics together? On Sundays?"

Samantha closes her eyes. "Oh, Daddy," she says, "my sentimental daddy."

"Sentimental daddy?"

"His life is falling apart, he can't quite get it right, he's failing here and he's failing there—but, by golly, does he love his little girl."

I want to say, *Don't talk that way to me*, but what comes out is, "I do. I mean, love you."

Samantha laughs and opens her door. "Let's pick up these newspapers," she says.

"Good idea," I say.

And we do: we pick up the newspapers from the driveway, several of which date back from last week, and one from last month, a Sunday edition soggily encased within its wrapper, whose exterior bears the number of a lawn service I really should call. We carry the newspapers inside, where Samantha begins throwing them into the kitchen trashcan I still haven't gotten the right size bags for, when I say, "Don't. Not yet." Samantha shoots me a disapproving look. I retrieve a few newspapers from the trash, unburden them of their comics section, and place the remainder back in the can. "There," I say. I set the comics on the kitchen table, which still holds a few cereal boxes I've being meaning to flatten since forever. Should ask the knit cap kid to stomp them, I think, the moment before Samantha sits down at the table and begins reading the comics aloud the way she used to when she was a child, Julie and I flanking each side of her, helping Samantha with the few words she didn't know. Samantha reads *The Family Circus*, where a legion of dotted lines trails Billy's quest for his lost baseball mitt; then *Peanuts,* where Snoopy's mustachioed brother, Spike, is lost in a desert populated by fat cacti, to *Blondie*, where Dagwood has forgotten his lunchbox again, apostrophes of sweat radiating from his worried brow.

That night I stay awake and listen for Samantha to turn off her bedroom light. That's something I always do, something that would only prove to Samantha how much of a sentimental daddy I really am, and something I am glad she does not know about. After Samantha shuts off the light, I permit myself to fall asleep. I dream that I'm riding Question Man's bicycle through my neighborhood. Houses speed by, and I know one of them is mine, but for the life of me, I cannot tell which one.

————

The first time I met Question Man was the week Julie moved out. I was out getting the mail, whose envelopes wished to rebuke me with Julie's name—Julie always got more mail than me, catalogs, mostly, but still—when Question Man pedaled by, his boom box blaring Willie Nelson. I turned to look at him, because how could you not turn to look at a full-grown man wearing a Lycra tracksuit singing "Born to Lose" very, very badly? You couldn't. Question Man waved, and nearly crashed into the low hedge that borders my driveway, the one that is presently overgrown, in need of a significant trim, and freckled with empty beer cans. I waved back, a gesture Question Man always reads as an invitation to talk, but I did not know that yet, and so was surprised when Question Man doubled back and came to a halt beside the mailbox. His eyes were red and raw looking. His smile was a dropped jack o'lantern.

"Is this about Julie?" he asked. "Because I could understand that, if this was something about Julie."

Figuring Question Man to be some kind of neighborhood crank, someone whom Julie had spoken to in the past, perhaps, I said, "Is what about Julie?"

"This," Question Man said, and waved his arms as if to indicate my home, my driveway, my neighborhood, and what I now understand to mean, in Question Man parlance, *me*. My situation. My life.

"I'm not sure I understand," I said.

Question Man said, "Does anyone?" and pedaled away.

The morning after the recital, Julie calls to tell me Jimmy Carter has left her. I ask her what does she mean, and she says what do I think she means and bursts into tears. She says she had no idea it was coming. She doesn't know what to do. She's in hell right now, that where she is, do I know what she means? I recall those first weeks after the separation, alone in the house, me sleeping in the living room, the family room, and a few times beneath the dining room table, whose upholstered chairs and heavy legs temporarily gave me the feeling of sentinels standing guard, keeping loneliness at bay.

"Do you know where he went?" I ask.

"No," Julie cries. "Probably to his goddamn golf game, that's where. Jesus, this is so fucking embarrassing." She cries the way she did when we were splitting up. Julie and me loading boxes into the U-Haul she rented for the day, even though I said I'd be glad to drive the rest over in my Civic.

"Did he take the Hummer?"

Julie says, "What do you mean, did he take the Hummer?"

"Well, I just meant, does he have it or do you have it, is all?"

"Why would that matter?"

"Well," I say, and know I'm about to say something I'm going to later regret, "I was just thinking that if you had the Hummer, you could drive it over here and you know, just sort of hang out until you figure out what's next."

"Jesus, Tom," Julie says. "When will you ever learn?"

That afternoon, Samantha tells me we're going to clean out the house. For good, she says, and hands me a trash bag and an empty box. "Start cleaning," Samantha says, but I say I don't know where to start. Samantha looks around the house. We're standing between the kitchen and dining room, the dining room table stacked to the chandelier with children's board games and puzzles, the breakfront sheltering three or four dozen stuffed animals, each kitchen chair wearing several layers of children's sweaters and winter coats—even, I now notice, the one that Samantha first learned to zipper all by herself, as she did one rainy afternoon when I picked her up late from daycare, forgetting an umbrella, and needing to hide her butterfly watercolor beneath my jacket, the painting still magnetized to my refrigerator today.

"Do you want to know how to find a good place to start?" Samantha asks. "Step one: close your eyes. Step two: point. Step three: open your eyes and begin throwing crap away."

"I wish you wouldn't say 'crap.'"

Samantha hands me an angle broom. "Let's give me nothing to talk about," she says.

"Okay," I say. "Deal."

We start cleaning. We clean everywhere. We carry things to my car. We stand before the little red and blue play table with the little play hammers and the little play drill, and then we lift the little red and blue play table and carry it out to my Civic, the play tools swinging, and load the thing into my trunk, barely wide enough to accept the table's colorful width. I toss an inflatable rocking horse into the back seat until Samantha reminds me to deflate it first, which I do, watching the horse's hopeful smile collapse into a sunken grin. Samantha fills box after box with board books, and sets them by the front door for me to carry to the car, which I don't mind doing, especially since it gives me a chance to rescue *Goodnight, Moon* and *The Runaway Bunny* and hide them behind a planter. Sentimental daddy, Samantha would say. What's wrong with a little sentimentality, this daddy would like to know, this realist, this doer, this get-the-job-doner, this nose-to-the-grindstoner: see him there stuffing the glove compartment with ballet shoes. Watch him fit another Cabbage Patch Kid into the space between the wheel well and spare tire. Is he really going to strap an oversized stuffed giraffe to the top of the Civic—he is! See him tie the beast down.

"That's going to fall off," Samantha says.

"I used three bungee cords."

"I'll just hold on to him," Samantha says, and unclasps the cords, which, now that she mentions it, were sort of loose, I admit it.

We climb into the car, which takes some doing. I forgot that human beings would need to fit into the car, too, as Samantha and I must, our knees to the dashboard (Samantha) and the steering wheel (me), a wicker changing table blocking the rear view, which, in the moment we back away, includes Question Man, whom I narrowly miss with my taillight, and who shouts over Gene Krupa's tribal tom-toms, "Is this about Julie and Jimmy Carter?" I give him a look that intends to say, *Go away, now,* but fear I've given him one that says, *We'll be back in hour for the next load.* As we're leaving the neighborhood, I can see Question Man following us in my side-view mirror. He's got the puppy in the front basket, his puppy tongue peeking from his puppy mouth. I'd tell Samantha to check out the puppy, but she's got her earbuds on again, plus she wouldn't look anyway, plus it takes me a minute to think about whether I should tell Samantha about the puppy or not, and by the time I do, we've left the neighborhood and Question Man behind.

We arrive at the consignment store—Cradle and All—where Samantha carries the play table though the doors first, me trailing behind, saying, Careful, don't scratch it, as Samantha rolls her eyes and says, Please. We take in several loads: toys and games, bags of onesies and footie pajamas, tap shoes, the wicker changing table, and the red and blue play table, of course, whose hammers I've been using lately, if you want to know the truth, a good way to pass the hours before sleep: drive a few willing pegs through a few willing holes, ah. The woman behind the register takes a liking to us, this father and daughter relinquishing the toys of the daughter's youth. She assembles the changing table in a flash, tests its drawers; she appraises the clothes in a matter of seconds. She tells us she can take everything, gives us a price. Hands me an invoice.

"Is that all?" I say.

"We'll take it," Samantha says.

"That's a really good play table," I protest. "I think we paid a lot for it."

"Don't listen to him," Samantha says, but the woman laughs and says she'll give us two dollars more for it, why not? Samantha says thanks and directs me back through the door and into my car before I can change my mind, she says, reading my thoughts the way she sometimes does. We're not even out of the parking lot before Julie calls me on my cell phone.

"I'm on the road," Julie says. "I should be back by lunchtime."

"By yourself?" I say. "I mean, is Jimmy with you?"

"Jimmy is not with me," Julie says, and I can hear her start to cry.

"Does he know you're coming back? I mean, did you talk to him?"

"Could you do me a favor, Tom?" Julie says. "Could you please stop asking me questions? Can't you see I don't want any questions right now? Can't you understand that?"

I want to tell her she has no idea how well I can understand that, especially as I spot Question Man bicycling into the parking lot as I pull out onto the highway. He gives me a questioning look, and shouts, "Did you sell the play table?" the moment I join the highway and tell Julie I will stop asking her questions.

"Promise?" Julie says.

"Promise," I say.

Samantha puts a finger to the passenger window and says, "Isn't that your friend? That weird fat guy?" but she says it loud enough for me to know she's got her iPod turned up loud and I don't need to answer. I do anyway. "Where?" I say but Samantha only says, "I feel sorry for the puppy."

Back home, we load up the car again. We drive the load to Cradle and All, and then the second load becomes a third load, and then the third becomes the fourth, and then Samantha and I decide to grab some lunch before our next load. I'm fine with Subway, but Samantha has a thing against fast food. We settle on a cafe near the consignment store, a place I've gone by a thousand times without ever noticing. Not my kind of place, really, but Samantha is excited by the menu, which is chalked above the cash register and seems heavy on sprouts. I order a bagel with smoked salmon (I wanted bacon) and Samantha gets a burrito that comes out looking like an avocado-stuffed bean bag. We eat our food in silence until Question Man shows up, huffing and puffing, and orders the bagel with cream cheese and bacon. A V of sweat shows through his shirt. His hair is sticking up to one side. When he sits down across from us, Samantha gives me a look and says, "What's the deal with him, anyway?"

I am about to answer when Question Man says hello to Samantha, and asks me, "Why didn't you get the bacon?"

"He's trying to cut back," Samantha explains.

Question Man gives me a questioning look and says, "Is that what this is about? Cutting back?"

On our sixth and final load to the consignment store, Samantha lifts the toy piano from her bedroom and carries it to the car. "Not the toy piano," I say, but Samantha places it at her feet and pulls her seatbelt on.

"Come on," she says, "drive."

"You can't be serious," I say. I remind her that the toy piano was a gift from her mom and me, the gift that got her started on piano, the gift that showed Samantha her own.

"Drive," Samantha says.

"But."

"Drive."

And I do. I drive to the consignment store, where it shouldn't surprise me to see Julie waiting in the parking lot, Jimmy Carter's Hummer angrily glinting in the sunlight, Julie shielded behind tinted glass, her sunglasses masking tears I won't see until she steps from the Hummer and hugs

Samantha, who, in the moment before she opens her door, explains to me that she called Julie when I was loading the car, told her we'd be here, that she should meet us here in this dismal parking lot, which, as I pull into it, includes Question Man, pedaling his puppy bike in front of Cradle and All. None of these things should surprise me, but they do. They surprise me as much my tears, those inexplicable visitors, those sudden guests, whose presence I wipe away before Samantha notices.

"I think Mom needs me," Samantha says, matter-of-factly.

"Yeah," I say.

"She can't handle this alone."

Who can? I want to say, but what comes out is, "I know."

Before Samantha closes her door, she says, "Don't forget to get rid of the piano."

I don't say anything, and Samantha knows what I'm thinking, which is that I'll keep the piano and buy back her other stuff, too, but Samantha strikes a deal with me. "Throw it out, and I'm done with 'Skidamarink,'" she says. "For good."

"Really?"

"Really."

"Okay," I say, and for a moment, that's how I feel, until Julie and Samantha pull away in Jimmy Carter's Hummer and Question Man pedals up to me. He leans his bike against a streetlight without locking it, the puppy loosely bungeed into the basket. I'm about to carry Samantha's toy piano into the consignment store, when Question Man says, "Is that what this is all about? Samantha's toy piano?"

I turn to look at him. He is wearing a vinyl poncho and a grease-stained baseball cap, the cap's logo coming unstitched, difficult to read. His shoe-laces are made of yarn. The puppy's eyes are crusted with yellow goo.

"Yes, this is about Samantha's toy piano," I say.

Question Man gives me a look. "And what about Anne?" he says. "Is this about Anne, too?"

I thrust the toy piano at him. Question Man catches it awkwardly, the keys sounding an off-key chord. "Yes, this is about Anne," I say.

Question Man grins his joyless grin. "And Samantha's rocking chair? And the Sunday comics?"

I grab Question Man by the collar. "Yes, this is about the Sunday comics," I say. "It's always been about the Sunday comics."

"And the divorce?" Question Man asks, but his voice sounds funny—a little strained—but it isn't until I've dropped him to his knees that I realize it's because I'm twisting his collar into a knot.

"Yes, this is about the divorce!" I say. "It's always been about the divorce! And Samantha and Julie and Jimmy Carter!" I twist the knot tighter. "And the play table and Skidamarink! It's about all of that! Everything!" Question Man drops the piano to the ground, its lid breaking free, splintering into a dozen pieces. "That's what this is all about—*everything*!"

Question Man smiles and asks me a question, but I don't know what it is and never will, for I steal his bike and begin pedaling for my life, pumping one leg and then the other, until I've left the parking lot behind and let this foolish dog eye me from his foolish basket and know that I will never give him back, not eventually, not ever.

A POSSIBLE THING

The first time Jonas's father let him mow the lawn, Jonas made an embarrassing mistake. This was the summer Jonas turned nine, the summer his father moved to an apartment across town, but still ate dinner with Jonas and his mother, still remodeled the bathroom he'd been promising to finish for years, and still did all of the yard work, a series of rituals that both confused and clarified Jonas's notion of the world. His father was still has father and his family was still his family—except for how they weren't. Jonas's father had been mowing the front yard when Jonas's mother sent him outside to help. Jonas knew this was a rouse to get him out of the house, *to get him motivated*, as she sometimes said.

It was hot outside. Jonas stood in the driveway, kicking pebbles onto the lawn. Jonas's father wore his T-shirt tucked into his shorts, white sneakers, and a baseball cap.

When he reached the end of the yard, he turned around and spotted Jonas. Jonas wasn't sure whether or not to wave, but did anyway. His father waved back. A moment later, he gave Jonas a glance that said, *I'm surprised to see you out here.* Jonas tried to summon a face that said, *I'm here to help,* but feared he'd registered one that said, *Mom sent me.* His father was mowing the yard horizontally, Jonas remembered, for the embarrassing thing depended on it. His father cut the engine and approached the driveway, where Jonas stood with his hands in his pockets. Why could he never stop putting his hands in his pockets?

"Hey there," his father said.

"Hey."

"You look a little bored." His father offered him a look to let Jonas know that this wasn't a criticism; he was being conspiratorial with him. His socks were shagged with grass. "Boring day."

"Maybe."

"Hot enough," his father said. "That's for sure."

"Yeah." Jonas knew his father was only trying to make him feel at ease, to draw him into some friendly chitchat, but Jonas was lousy at chitchat. He couldn't quite get a handle on adult conversation, somehow. Adult conversation was like trying to steer a shopping cart from the opposite end.

"Did Mom send you out here?"

Jonas felt his face grow warm. "Maybe."

"Maybe," his father said. Then, "Just between you and me, she's been sending me out here for years." His father gave Jonas another look, one that said, *It's okay to laugh. I'm letting you in on a tradition of fathers and sons speaking of women as if they're bossy, even though you know we don't really think so.*

"Yeah," Jonas said. "She told me to help you."

His father considered this. "Well," he said, "I guess you should help me, then."

Jonas's father would start the mower for him, he explained, since it was sometimes tough to get going and unsafe for a nine-year-old, even one as strong as him. "You take this cord and give it a good pull, like a backwards punch," his father said, gripping the T-topped starter, and glancing over his shoulder where Jonas stood, nodding, knowing his father was pleased to explain this to him, his enjoyment obvious, easy to read. His father pulled the cord. The engine started instantly. "Now, put your hands on the handle. Good. You feel how it shakes? That's why you need to keep a good grip on the safety bar. Right. Like that. Let go and the engine will cut out. It's so you don't get the bright idea to check under the blade while it's running. Got it?"

Jonas nodded.

"Try to line up the wheels as straight as you can. The idea is to follow the lines."

"Okay."

"If you want, you can line up the wheels an inch or two outside mine. Might be easier."

"Okay."

"But you do what you think best."

Jonas aligned the wheels along the left hand margin of uncut grass.

"Good," his father said. "Keep going."

And Jonas did. He kept going across the front lawn, the mower shaking beneath his grip, but nothing too bad. There wasn't much to it, after all, mowing the lawn. Jonas followed the mower across the middle of the yard, which sloped downwards more than he had realized before. Mowing was simple, the lawn would have him know. Something a kid could do. This news saddened Jonas. Maybe everything would be the same way, a disappointment. Terrible thought. To dispel it, Jonas imagined that his father was cheering him on, although he knew he was just watching him from the driveway.

Jonas followed the line. He tried to keep one set of wheels an inch or two just outside his father's line since this seemed to make things easier, no room for error. A grass catcher grew off the side of the mower, a fat canvas bag with a thick zipper that trembled when Jonas steered the mower around the sewer run-out. Jonas navigated this, as he did the lone pine branch hanging across the property line, whose bough required him to duck without losing his grip on the safety handle. How thrilling it was to pass underneath the branch, the mower too high for the short grass that grew there, its blades spinning free. Jonas headed toward the property line.

And then Jonas made his mistake. He neared the property line—an invisible line, Jonas would have anyone know, if they'd like to tease him about it, as insubstantial as the Mason-Dixon—knowing that he should stop, that stopping and turning was what one did when one mowed, as his father had done when he'd wheeled the mower to the driveway, but unable to shake the idea that the mower would direct him what to do. The mower would turn itself around. And even though Jonas would not like to admit that these were his thoughts, so childish and dumb and naive, with their ardent wish to confer consciousness upon a lawn mower, whose head was filled with gasoline, no more sentient than the stuffed animals

Jonas sometimes received as gifts and grudgingly attached names to, these were his thoughts as he crossed the property line, his grip firm, no looking back.

Jonas mowed into the neighbor's yard.

Jonas mowed into the neighbor's yard and kept going.

Jonas didn't know how to turn the mower around.

It would have been a story told about him, a family story, joining all the other family stories, repeated, perhaps, during holidays and car trips, at weddings and gatherings, at Christmas and Thanksgiving, or their annual trip to Rehoboth Beach, where Jonas's grandfather rented a house that stood on wood pilings and had a lawn comprised of white stones that taunted Jonas's feet, home from another shapeless day of running through the green-gray surf, where dolphins could sometimes be glimpsed, sudden fermatas above the waves, as small planes carried banners through the sky. SATISFY YOUR SWEET TOOTH AT DOLLE'S!!

Had the story become a story, Jonas might have found himself sitting at his grandfather's too-high table, where his grandmother was setting a grocery bag of steamed crabs onto a serving dish while his Aunt Franny tonged an ear of corn onto Jonas's plate, the corn also steaming, still wearing a few threads of silk. Someone might break the silence with a joke, someone like Uncle Neil, especially Uncle Neil, who might turn a bulging mouthful of cole slaw toward him and say, "Guess they don't have much of a lawn for you to mow down here, do they?"

Grins, people laughing. His mother telling Uncle Neil he's *bad*—but laughing, too.

"Hell, Neil, Jonas doesn't need a lawn," his grandfather might say, "when he's got the neighbors.'"

"You got that right," Uncle Neil would say, as one of Jonas's cousins, probably Susan, would pat him on the back, even though this gesture would be public and intended for laughs, Jonas trying to be a good sport, as Aunt Franny announced, to the youngest cousins, "You've all heard that story, right? About the time Uncle Dan was trying to teach Jonas how to mow the lawn?" and the cousins, pretending they hadn't already heard the story the last time the family was together, would say *No, what happened?* kicking cousin Jess under the table the moment he opened his big dumb mouth and started to say, "He kept on going."

If it was a story all of these things might have come to pass, but it was not a story. It was not a story because Jonas's father never told anyone. Instead he followed Jonas into the neighbor's yard and stopped him with a tap on the shoulder. "Hey," he said, loudly, but not a shout. "You okay?"

This question, coupled with his father's expression, was Jonas's first understanding that he'd begun to cry. "Yeah," he said.

"What do you say we turn this thing around?"

Jonas nodded. How could he have begun to cry?

"What we'll want to do is push down on the handle. Good. That's it. Both hands."

Jonas felt his father's hands on his own, guiding him.

"And now we'll just go back the way we came." His father positioned the mower in the row of cut grass, not wanting, Jonas understood, to double his mistake. They'd leave as little trace as possible. "See? You knew how to do it all along."

"Yeah," Jonas said, forgetting to raise his voice.

"You knew," his father said. "But the mower had other ideas."

Jonas knew his father was only trying to cheer him. He'd seen his tears, after all, those stupid tears.

"Sometimes this mower gets ideas."

They'd pushed the mower back to their yard, Jonas's father taking over from there. Jonas followed him around for a while, his father letting him try his hand at mowing beneath the azaleas. His father's advice: don't worry about making it perfect. Just get as much as you can. You can always finish up with the trimmer later.

The night of the mowing, Jonas's mother allowed them to eat dinner in front of television. His father sat at one end of the sofa and folded his pizza in half, the way he always claimed real New Yorkers did. His father grew up outside of Syracuse, in a town they once drove through, on a family vacation Jonas could hardly recall, aside from the hand-held video game he'd been permitted to take along, whose music still recalled gray factories issuing gray smoke, and a fenced-in pedestrian bridge where Jonas glimpsed two boys spitting onto passing cars.

"So," his mother said, after a while. "I heard you had quite an adventure today."

"Yeah," Jonas said. On television, Hawkeye Pierce was trying to trick Frank Burns into doing something you knew was going to humiliate him, but was going to be funny, anyway.

"Got his first taste of mowing the lawn," his father said. "A real pro." He laughed his surprising laugh. His dad thought Hawkeye Pierce was just about the funniest thing.

Jonas's mother didn't say anything. Silence loomed. On the screen, Hawkeye gave Frank a mock salute, then kissed him on the cheek.

"Ha," his Jonas's father said. "Saw that coming."

"Right on da kisser," Jonas said. Sometimes he felt like they all talked more like television when the television was on.

"He got him on the cheek," his mother said.

"Still," his father said.

"Yeah," Jonas said. "Still." He gave his father a look that said, *Thanks for not telling*, but whether his father returned the look with one that said, *No problem*, Jonas could not tell. What was clear was that his father was never going to tell his mother about him mowing into the neighbor's yard. He was never going to tell anyone about seeing tears in his eyes, since telling would only be humiliating to Jonas and since not telling drew them closer together, father and son, son and family. It would become a secret. Jonas and his father would share a secret.

Forever.

In the weeks before he moved out of the house for good, Jonas's father dragged the trashcans back to the garage, even though he'd done nothing to fill them. He installed a basketball backboard that Jonas's grandparents had gotten him, but never took a shot. He restacked the woodpile while Jonas tried out the new balsa glider they'd gotten from the supermarket. His father was more willing to buy him things like that since moving out, Jonas noticed, without any sense of pleasure, though. The plane had a single propeller upon which a rubber band could be hooked, the rubber band knotting with a strange intensity as Jonas dared to wind it to its near breaking point, something the instructions had warned against.

The plane, tossed from Jonas's hand, veered sharply to the right and dove into the lawn. The wing broke off and refused to fit back into place. Jonas explained the problem to his father.

"You don't need to throw it so hard," his father said, taking the plane in hand and urging the wind back into place. "You'll get a lot more from a little," he said, and, in the expert way he had of matching phrase to action—*like a backwards punch*—took the plane, wound the propeller, and released it into the air like a rehabilitated pigeon. The plane ascended into the sky and floated across the yard. Sky Streak, the plane's wing read. "How was that?" his father said.

"Great," Jonas said.

"It was, wasn't it?" his father said. His tone wasn't boastful; he seemed genuinely surprised by his own good luck. There's some bluffing in being a parent, Jonas realized.

The last evening his father spent in the house, he cooked hamburgers on the grill, the one Jonas and his mother never used otherwise. "Need to refill the tank," his father said, but his mother didn't say anything. The three of them were seated around the picnic table on the back deck. His father forked a second burger onto Jonas's plate. "I could just run up to Casey's."

Jonas's mother took a sip of the iced tea his father had made earlier that day. He'd let Jonas squeeze lemon into the pitcher while he stirred it with a fork. "That's okay," she said.

"I bet Jonas would like going to Casey's," his father said. Jonas glanced him from the corner of his eye and felt the air thicken around them. "He's always liked going to Casey's."

"Yeah," Jonas concurred.

Jonas's mother shook her head. "That's all right," she said.

Jonas's father sat down at the table with them and took a bite of potato salad. "Tank's on its last legs. One refill will last you the rest of summer."

"We're fine," his mother maintained. She glanced off to the neighbor's yard. Jonas wasn't sure where to look, since he sensed the conversation just beginning to veer off course, the Sky Streak improperly thrown.

"You sure?" His father sipped his iced tea. "Easy enough to go to Casey's."

Jonas looked at his mother, but she kept her head turned away. "We could all go to Casey's," he chanced. "Together."

His mother stood from the table and placed her napkin on her plate. "We're not going to Casey's," she said. A breeze blew the napkin off the deck, but his mother neglected to retrieve it. She left Jonas and his father at the table, where green flies treaded the air above her plate.

After dinner, his father replaced a light bulb in the foyer closet, reset the microwave clock, and oiled the hinges on the laundry room doors. Later, they all sat and watched television as the sky turned pink outside. Jonas observed it through the sliding glass doors. In them, he could see himself and his mother father, thrillingly framed within the door's reflection. He imagined someone peering in, seeing them and thinking nothing was out of the ordinary. The idea pleased him. Jonas knew his father would have to leave soon, but this knowledge hadn't seemed to reach his father yet, the reflection let Jonas know: his father had his arms stretched across the back of the sofa, a kid allowed up past his bedtime.

After a while, Jonas's mother said, "It's getting late," but no one said anything. His father looked at his watch—the watch Jonas was sometimes permitted to shake, winding it, tricking time into obedience—and made a noise Jonas couldn't decipher. "Well," he said.

"It's almost eight," his mother said.

His father placed his arms across his lap, but made no motion to move.

"It's been a long afternoon," his mother continued. "For everyone." Outside, a gray moth blundered into the sliding glass doors. The television cast blue-green light across the room.

"Okay," his father said. "Let's call it a night, then."

But, when Jonas returned downstairs a few moments later, after pretend-brushing his teeth and lingering at the top of the stairs, his father was outside on the deck, crouched before the grill. Approaching, Jonas saw that he'd moved the propane tank, although the tank was still connected to the grill.

"Stuck," his father explained, spotting him.

"Oh."

"I thought I had it for a second, but…" his voice trembled with effort. "It doesn't want to budge."

"Where's Mom?"

His father shrugged. "Upstairs. Or maybe on a walk."

"Does she know you're still here?"

His father nodded. "She does."

"Oh."

There was a place on his father's head where hair no longer grew that Jonas observed with sudden interest: how rarely one saw the top of one's parents' heads.

"You going to bed?" his father asked.

"I guess."

"You sure?"

"Yeah."

His father nodded. "Well, if you're sure." He extended his hand, which was slick with sweat. "Goodnight."

"Goodnight."

But Jonas found himself unable to leave. He stood in the kitchen and watched his father wrestle the propane tank from its mooring. Where was his mother? Sometimes she took a flashlight walk through the neighborhood, something she'd done for years without striking Jonas as the least bit strange, although now he saw something else in these solo walks, these temporary leavings, which seemed to contain the seeds of his parents' separation, as hard and clear and piercing as the bulb within the flashlight's head.

"There we go," his father said. "Got it." He turned to Jonas without conveying the least bit of surprise that Jonas was still there. "But give the old tank credit; she really put up a fight."

"Yeah."

"Next time I won't tighten it so much. Lesson learned."

It occurred to Jonas that his father was only talking to prolong this evening. To hold back another lonely drive to his apartment complex, where Jonas had left a few of his least-liked action figures, in case of emergency boredom.

"Hey," his father said. "You want to go with me to Casey's?"

"Mom said no."

But his father didn't say anything. Instead he handed the propane tank to Jonas, which was heavier than Jonas has imagined, where a rusty valve stared indifferently at him, this kid with pale skinny arms clutching an empty tank like an unwanted carnival prize.

"You can put that in the back seat," his father said. "Car's unlocked."

"But."

"We'll be back before she knows we're gone," his father said, as if this were a possible thing. A thing as likely as the lawnmower turning itself around. As possible as anything you might wish for.

They pulled out of the driveway with the propane tank seat-belted into the backseat, the neighborhood on the edge of darkness, Jonas's heart beating in his ears. What would his mother say? "I bet you didn't think we'd be going off an adventure tonight, huh?" his father said. He'd rolled the windows down. *An adventure*, his father's phrase for church services, dentist appointments, grandparent visits, drive-thru banking, and every other dull enterprise since Jonas was a toddler. The wind took Jonas's hair. Outside, houses passed by, their lawns dimly green in the streetlight. "Let's get some air in here."

Jonas rested his arm against the passenger window. "We should have left a note," he said. "For mom."

His father said, "Beautiful night."

It was. A fat moon presided above a sky freckled with stars. The wind held the scent of damp honeysuckle. The post office parking lot, empty at this time of night, seemed unnecessarily important, urgent, the secret to everything Jonas did not know. And then it passed in an instant, its secret kept, and Jonas was returned to the ordinariness of his father turning the radio on. It got darker out. A car, turning ahead of them, was two red lights subsumed by a stand of pine.

"You'll need to figure out the trimmer," Jonas's father said. "Soon enough."

"Yeah," Jonas said. "I know."

"It's not too hard. The tricky part is replacing the spool. There's a notch you've got to feed the wire through, otherwise it won't feed out when you bump it."

"Okay," Jonas said. Feed the wire through. Bump it. He had no idea what his father was talking about, but understood his job was to agree, to assent, to let his father know he could move on to his apartment and his single life without forfeiting Jonas's love. Jonas would take care of things back home. He would mow the yard and trim the grass around the front porch. He would not mow into the neighbor's yard, whose embarrassing tracks were already being covered, Jonas realized, the grass growing over them, a notion that pleased him, and gave him confidence enough to ask his father how to replace the mower's spark plug.

His father told him.

"And what about replacing the air filter?"

The air filter was the easiest of all, his father said, something he would only need to do once at the beginning of the season. The rest of the summer, Jonas could just clean it out after every other mowing or so, depending on how dry the grass was. The dryer the grass, the dirtier the filter. Which reminded his father: get in the habit of watering the lawn in the morning, never in the evening. Wear gloves when weeding the flowerbeds along the driveway. Watch the vines that cling to the underside of the air conditioner; get them at the roots or they'll never lose their grip. Scrape dried grass from the mower bed with a screwdriver. Change your mowing pattern every time. Never mow the same way twice. Set the mower wheels at the middle height. You only want to cut the top third of the grass, not the bottom. Cut the bottom third and the lawn will be brown by August.

Jonas asked his father about circuit breakers and fuses. He asked him about the attic above the stairs, where a string hung down just out of reach, and where he'd always been forbidden to enter, although he'd always wondered what was up there. Not much, his father told him, but he'd take him up there next week when he stopped by to get a few things. He had a sports locker up there with some pretty good baseball gloves he'd leave behind for Jonas, although his father did not say *leave behind*; he said, *For you to take care of*, which Jonas did not forget, when, the following week, he did accompany his father into the attic—scary, the threat of bees, exposed nails—and they looted the locker, which also held his father's old swimming trophies, also left behind, and also something for Jonas to take care of.

It was late when they got to Casey's. Jonas's father must have taken the propane tank from the back seat, and Jonas must have followed him inside, for Jonas remembered the feeling of the air-conditioned air inside Casey's, preposterously cold, as well as the candy aisle, from which Jonas was permitted to select a Kit Kat bar which Jonas ate on the drive home, where he and his father did not speak as they had on the way there, did not review the best way to get water out of the basement after a thunderstorm, as Jonas would later have to learn (you use the push broom to send it out the basement door) or how to reset the garbage disposal (there's a switch beneath the sink) or what it meant when the toilet kept running, even when Jonas replenished the water in the top tank and watched the little ball impaled upon a rubber rod rise to the FULL line (it meant it was time to replace the universal kit, easy enough to do once you shut the valve off). They must have talked about something. Of course they did, what with the errand accomplished and the candy bar to split between them and the need to get home before Jonas's mother returned, that impossible possibility that had sent them off into the night in the first place. They must have said something when they pulled up into the driveway and carried the propane tank to the deck, where Jonas's father hooked it up to the grill, the one Jonas and his mother would use the rest of the summer, the two of them keeping an eye on the hotdogs and burgers they could never get to come out the way Jonas's father did, just right, slightly blackened without being burnt. Or course they must have talked about something.

But Jonas will not remember the drive home. He does not want to remember it, and so he will not. Instead, he will imagine the drive to Casey's over and over again, usually on nights when he fears he's let the grass grow too high and cannot sleep, or hears his mother's weeping through the wall that separates his bedroom from hers. He will recall the wind in his hair, the propane tank seat-belted into the back seat. The tank made a tiny noise when they went over a bump in the road, something that terrified Jonas—would the tank explode?—although he didn't say anything to his father, even when they pulled into Casey's and dipped into the parking lot and the tank made the noise again. That's the end of the story for Jonas, the tank making the noise, but with no consequences. They pull into the parking lot and go inside. No harm comes their way. No misfortune. No problems.

Because that's what the story is for Jonas: a story about a boy and his father driving in the night. The moon is out, the stars gorgeous. They have an errand to run, and so they are running it. They drive and drive, never to return. There is no other possibility.

TITLES FROM ELIXIR PRESS

POETRY

Circassian Girl by Michelle Mitchell-Foust

Imago Mundi by Michelle Mitchell-Foust

Distance From Birth by Tracy Philpot

Original White Animals by Tracy Philpot

Flow Blue by Sarah Kennedy

A Witch's Dictionary by Sarah SarKennedy

The Gold Thread by Sarah Kennedy

Rapture by Sarah Kennedy

Monster Zero by Jay Snodgrass

Drag by Duriel E. Harris

Running the Voodoo Down by Jim McGarrah

Assignation at Vanishing Point by Jane Satterfield

Her Familiars by Jane Satterfield

The Jewish Fake Book by Sima Rabinowitz

Recital by Samn Stockwell

Murder Ballads by Jake Adam York

Floating Girl (Angel of War) by Robert Randolph

Puritan Spectacle by Robert Strong

X-testaments by Karen Zealand

Keeping the Tigers Behind Us by Glenn J. Freeman

Bonneville by Jenny Mueller

State Park by Jenny Mueller

Cities of Flesh and the Dead by Diann Blakely

Green Ink Wings by Sherre Myers

Orange Reminds You Of Listening by Kristin Abraham

In What I Have Done & What I Have Failed To Do by Joseph P. Wood

Bray by Paul Gibbons

The Halo Rule by Teresa Leo

Perpetual Care by Katie Cappello

The Raindrop's Gospel: The Trials of St. Jerome and St. Paula by Maurya Simon

Prelude to Air from Water by Sandy Florian

Let Me Open You A Swan by Deborah Bogen

Cargo by Kristin Kelly

Spit by Esther Lee

Rag & Bone by Kathrym Nuernberger

Kingdom of Throat-stuck Luck by George Kalamaras

Mormon Boy by S. Brady Tucker

Nostalgia for the Criminal Past by Kathleen Winter

Little Oblivion by Susan Allspaw

Quelled Communiqués by Chloe Joan Lopez

Stupor by David Ray Vance

Curio by John Nieves

The Rub by Ariana-Sophia Kartsonis

Visiting Indira Gandhi's Palmist by Kirun Kapur

Freaked by Liz Robbins

Looming by Jennifer Franklin

Flammable Matter by Jacob Victorine

Prayer Book of the Anxious by Josephine Yu

flicker by Lisa Bickmore

Sure Extinction by John Estes

State Park by Jenny Mueller

Selected Proverbs by Michael Cryer

Rise and Fall of the Lesser Sun Gods by Bruce Bond

I will not kick my friends by Kathleen Winter

FICTION

How Things Break by Kerala Goodkin

Juju by Judy Moffat

Grass by Sean Aden Lovelace

Hymn of Ash by George Looney

Nine Ten Again by Phil Condon

Memory Sickness by Phong Nguyen

Troglodyte by Tracy DeBrincat

The Loss of All Lost Things by Amina Gautier

The Killer's Dog by Gary Fincke

Everyone Was There by Anthony Varallo